THE
FAIRY
TALE
BOOK

Illustrated by Lisa Jackson
Adapted by Liz Scoggins

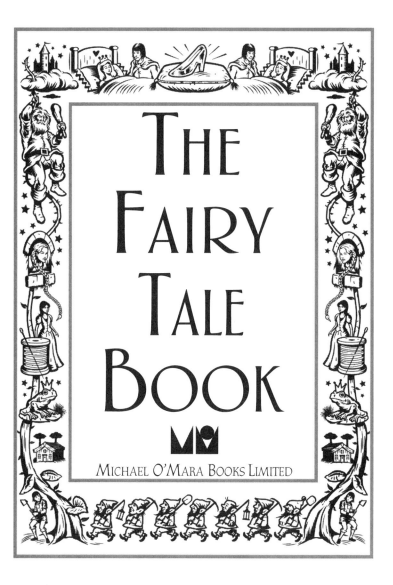

THE
FAIRY
TALE
BOOK

MICHAEL O'MARA BOOKS LIMITED

First published in Great Britain in 2009 by
Michael O'Mara Books Limited
9 Lion Yard, Tremadoc Road, London SW4 7NQ

Cover design by Zoe Quayle
Cover image by Paul Moran

A CIP catalogue record for this book is available from the British Library.

Papers used by Michael O'Mara Books Limited are natural, recyclable products made from wood grown in sustainable forests. The manufacturing processes conform to the environmental regulations of the country of origin.

ISBN 978-1-84317-335-9

1 3 5 7 9 10 8 6 4 2

www.mombooks.com

Printed and bound in Finland by WS Bookwell, Juva

Contents

Introduction

Each of the fairy tales in this collection has been especially chosen for its magical and mysterious qualities. You will discover many favourite characters and wonderful new friends, whose stories are sure to delight and amaze you. From beautiful princesses to scary giants, the perfect story is certainly waiting for you within the pages of this book.

The Artist

Lisa Jackson originally studied classical animation at Senior College Ballyfermot before moving into graphic design and comic books. She now concentrates on illustrating books for children in a variety of media, and lives and works in Dublin, Ireland.

The Frog Prince

One fresh spring evening, a beautiful Princess was strolling through the woods in the palace gardens, singing softly to herself. After some time, she arrived at a pretty pool, and decided to stay a little while.

The Princess had taken her favourite toy with her: a ball made of glistening gold. Over and over again, she threw the ball up into the air, catching it each time with a smile.

Her success made her confident, so she threw the ball into the air much higher than before. This time, the Princess did not catch it, and the ball dropped to the ground, and rolled straight into the water. When she peered into the pool, the poor girl found that the water was so deep she couldn't even see the bottom. The ball was nowhere to be seen. The Princess cried out, 'My favourite toy! I would give up everything if only I could get it back somehow.'

As she spoke, a little frog hopped out of the pool and asked the Princess why she was so upset. 'Why should you care, little frog?' she asked bitterly. 'My golden ball has fallen into the water, and now I'll never get it back.'

The frog thought for a moment and then said, 'If you promise to always love me, and let me live with you in the palace, I will get it back for you. You would only have to let me eat from your plate and sleep on your pillow. You would not have to give up anything.'

Now the Princess, thinking that the frog would never be able to follow her back to the palace, saw no harm in allowing him to fetch the ball. 'Very well,' she sniffed. The frog leapt into the water. When he returned, the frog spat the ball out at her feet and smiled. The Princess snatched up her ball and ran off. Even when the frog called after her, to remind her of her promise, she did not stop.

The next evening at dinner there was a tell-tale sound from the palace steps. *Splish-splosh-splish-splosh.* A knock sounded at the door, and a familiar little voice called out,

> 'Princess, Princess, open the door,
> Your woodland love can wait no more.
> Remember your promise at the pool,
> Your royal honour is the golden rule.'

The Princess had forgotten the promise she had made to the frog, and looked at the King guiltily. 'What is the matter, child?' he asked. Sighing, the Princess replied, 'Yesterday, a horrid little frog made me promise that he could live here with me, if he got my ball back from the pool.'

'And did he?' asked the King.

'Yes,' said the Princess quietly.

'Then you must honour your promise as the frog says, child. Let him in.'

The Princess rose reluctantly from her chair and opened the door. *Splish-splosh-splish-splosh.* The little frog hopped to the table and leapt straight to the Princess's plate.

The Princess completely lost her appetite, and when the frog had eaten his fill he asked her to take him to her bedchamber. There she placed him on her pillow, and he fell straight to sleep. In the morning, the frog hopped back to the pool. The Princess breathed a sigh of relief, but that evening, to her horror, a tell-tale sound came up the palace steps again. *Splish-splosh-splish-splosh.* Then there was a knock at the door,

> 'Princess, Princess, open the door,
> Your woodland love can wait no more.
> Remember your promise at the pool,
> Your royal honour is the golden rule.'

That evening the frog ate from the Princess's plate and slept on her pillow again, then returned to the pool in the morning. On the third evening, exactly the same thing happened, but when the Princess opened her eyes in the morning the frog was gone. Instead, a handsome Prince stood at the side of her bed, waiting for her to wake. 'Where did you come from?' she asked in surprise.

'Long ago, I was enchanted by a wicked fairy to live the rest of my life as a frog, until an honourable Princess took pity on me. Unless the Princess allowed me to live with her, and eat from her plate, and sleep on her pillow for three nights in a row, I would remain a frog forever.

'Now that you have broken this terrible spell,' said the Prince, 'I would be honoured if you would marry me, and live with me in my castle on the other side of the forest.'

The Princess was astonished, but very relieved that the King had made her honour her promise to the frog. She smiled and said, 'Yes,' for she knew already that she loved the Prince, and would be happy to spend her life with him. After the ceremony, the Prince's faithful servant arrived to take the happy couple to the castle on the other side of the forest. The Princess said a fond farewell to her father, the King, knowing that she would be able to visit often, as he was so nearby. She set out for her new home with the Prince who had once lived as a frog, and they lived happily ever after.

Jack And The Beanstalk

Long ago, a widow and her son Jack lived in a small cottage with a tiny garden beside it. They kept a cow, and lived on the money they made from selling her milk. After many years, the cow began to give less and less milk. One day, she gave no milk at all, so Jack's mother sent him to market, saying, 'Sell her for the best price you can. We must find another way to make a living.'

Jack led the cow away, whistling cheerily, and took the market path. There he met a man, who greeted him and asked where he was taking the cow. 'I'm off to sell her at market, so that we can buy food for winter,' said Jack.

'Is that so?' said the man. Then holding out his hand he asked, 'Would you perhaps take these beans in payment for your cow?'

'No fear!' said Jack, who was really quite a sensible boy. 'She's worth far more than a handful of beans.'

'But these are magical beans,' the man exclaimed. 'Plant them tonight, and by morning you'll have a beanstalk that reaches right up to the sky.' Poor Jack could not resist, and took the beans from the man. He watched worriedly as the man led the cow away, whistling cheerily.

When Jack returned home to the cottage, his mother was most surprised to see him back so soon. 'What did you get for the cow, Jack?' she asked at once. He swallowed his nerves and held out the handful of beans. 'What's this?' his mother wailed. 'Where is the money for the cow?'

When Jack explained that he had met a man on the way to market, and that he had made a fine offer for their cow, his mother was furious. She threw the beans out of the window, and sent the boy to bed without a thing to eat.

The next day Jack realized that even though the sun must be up and shining, it was still very dark in his bedroom. He looked out of his window and gasped in surprise. At the side of the cottage an enormous beanstalk had grown, just as the man had said. Its leaves were huge, and blocked out the light of the sun. Bravely, Jack leaned out and pulled himself on to the beanstalk. It really did stretch up to the sky, and he wondered what he might find at the top. So he climbed and climbed, right up through the clouds.

At the very top Jack found a path. He was not about to stop now, so he took the path to find out where it led, and walked right up to a huge house where a tall woman sat.

'Hello,' said Jack. As he had been sent straight to bed without any food, and had set off without eating breakfast, he immediately asked, 'Do you have anything I could eat?' The woman laughed at his daring, and led him inside.

'You must be careful,' she warned. 'My husband is an ogre, and he'll have you for breakfast if he catches sight of you!'

So Jack followed her to the kitchen as quietly as he could, and quickly ate up the bread and cheese she gave him. Just as he was finishing, the whole house began to shake with the thud of footsteps. The ogre was home.

'Quick! Hide in here,' the woman cried. She pushed Jack inside a large oven and closed the door, so that the ogre wouldn't see him. Through the oven grate Jack glimpsed a giant of a man. The ogre filled the entire doorway and was frowning furiously. He sniffed at the air and bellowed, 'Fee-fi-fo-fum, I smell the blood of an Englishman!'

The ogre's wife assured him that no one else was there, and set breakfast on the table. When he had eaten, the ogre took out several bags of gold coins, and began to count. There was so much gold that halfway through he fell asleep, so Jack took his chance and crept out of the oven. He slipped a whole bag of coins from under the ogre's nose as he left, and ran back to the beanstalk as fast as he could. Jack let the bag of coins fall to the ground, and quickly slithered down the beanstalk after it.

Jack's mother was ever so pleased with the money he had brought home. The two of them lived very well on it for a while, but the coins ran out sooner than they imagined, so Jack decided to climb up the beanstalk again. When he arrived at the enormous house, the tall woman was sitting outside once more. 'Hello,' said Jack boldly. 'Do you have anything to eat?'

'Cheeky lad,' she grumbled. 'You're the same boy that was here before. My husband, the ogre, was missing a bag of gold coins after your last visit. You'd better be off, or he'll have you for breakfast.'

Jack offered to explain if he could have some food, so the woman took him into the house and gave him some bread and cheese. Just as he was nearly finished, the house began to shake with the thud of footsteps, as it had before. This time Jack ran straight for the oven without being told, and hid before the ogre could see him. Just as before, the ogre cried out, 'Fee-fi-fo-fum, I smell the blood of an Englishman!' but his wife assured him that they were alone, and they settled down to breakfast. This time when he had finished, the ogre called out for his hen and ordered it to lay. Each time he said, 'Lay,' the hen would lay a perfect golden egg.

Jack could not resist, and when the ogre fell asleep he sprinted off with the hen tucked under his arm. The bird squawked and clucked and made such a fuss that the ogre woke with a start. 'Where's my hen?' he bellowed in a rage. The ogre's wife came running, but it was already too late. Jack had disappeared down the beanstalk with the hen.

Jack's mother was ever so impressed by the hen's laying, but Jack was still not satisfied. A few days later, he climbed up to the clouds for a third time, and crept up to the enormous house. There he waited until the woman came outside, then he slipped into the kitchen and hid himself in the cooking pot. A few moments later, the whole house began to shake with the thud of the ogre's footsteps. 'Fee-fi-fo-fum, I smell the blood of an Englishman!' he roared.

'No, no!' cried his wife, sure that Jack could not be in the house this time. However, she thought she should check the oven just to be certain. It was lucky for Jack that he had hidden in the cooking pot, and the nervous boy sat there quietly while the ogre and his wife ate breakfast. When they had finished eating the ogre called for his golden harp, which he ordered to sing. It played him a beautiful lullaby until he fell into a restful sleep, and began to snore. Jack took his chance again, climbed out of the cooking pot, and scooped up the golden harp on his way to the door. 'Master, help me!' the harp called out in alarm. The ogre awoke with a loud grunt that shook the tiles from the roof, and he just caught sight of young Jack in the distance, running away with his golden harp.

If Jack had not gained such a good start, the ogre would soon have caught up with him. For the ogre was so tall that for each step he took, Jack had to take six. The boy rushed helter-skelter to the top of the beanstalk, clambering down the tangle of vines quicker than he ever had before.

The ogre was not so far behind him now, but he climbed much more slowly than Jack, because the beanstalk did not feel as though it would take his weight.

Jack reached the base of the beanstalk long before the ogre and ran into the cottage. 'Quick, Mother, fetch the axe!' Jack yelled. He took the wood-cutting axe from her and chopped at the base of the beanstalk again and again. Shudders shot up to the ogre's feet who, when he realized what was happening, gave a shout of alarm. Then the stalk broke in two, and the unfortunate ogre tumbled to the ground some distance away – dead.

When Jack showed his mother the golden harp he had brought back, she hugged him with delight. The two soon became rich by selling the golden eggs laid by the hen, and they lived very well.

Hansel And Gretel

At the edge of a large forest, a woodcutter lived with his children, Hansel and Gretel, and their stepmother. The family was very poor, and there was not enough food for all of them. The woodcutter worried what would become of them, but his wife was more practical, and not very fond of her stepchildren. She told her husband, 'In the morning, we'll take them out to the forest. They'll never find their way home, and things will be much easier.'

The woodcutter was horrified, but agreed to his wife's idea. He went to sleep with a heavy heart. Hansel and Gretel, who were too hungry to sleep, had heard the whole plan. Hansel knew he must act quickly so that he and his sister could find their way home. He crept out of the house and gathered as many little white stones from the garden as he could carry in his pockets. 'Don't worry, Gretel, all will be well,' he whispered, and they slept at last.

Before sunrise, the woodcutter's wife shook the two children awake, saying, 'Get up at once, it's time to collect wood from the forest.' She gave each child a piece of bread, and the family set off. As they walked, Hansel hung back from the rest, looking back at their little house. Each time he paused, Hansel's father urged him to hurry, not realizing that his son was dropping the little white stones on the ground to mark the route they took.

Once they were deep in the forest, the woodcutter sent the children off to gather fallen branches for a fire. They came back with their arms full and sat warming themselves, while their parents went to cut more wood. As the two children were so hungry, and the fire was so warm, they started to feel quite tired, and drifted off to sleep.

The sky was dark when Hansel and Gretel woke up. The woodcutter and his wife still hadn't returned, and Gretel wailed, 'How will we ever find our way home?'

Hansel, however, was calm and took his sister by the hand. 'Just look at how the little white stones gleam in the moonlight, Gretel,' and shining on the ground was a clear path home. They walked all night until they came to the house at the edge of the forest. Their stepmother was astonished to see them again, but the woodcutter was very relieved. He had felt so guilty that he hadn't slept a wink.

Life returned to normal at the edge of the forest, but it was not long until the woodcutter and his wife were worried again. 'We must take the children deeper into the forest this time,' complained the woodcutter's wife. The poor man could think of no argument against her. The children, who heard her words, knew they must act quickly once more. But when Hansel went to the door, he found it had been locked, and the key was nowhere to be found.

'Don't worry, Gretel,' he whispered. 'We will find a way home again somehow.'

In the morning, the children were shaken awake again and given a piece of bread each, which they put in their pockets. The bread was so small, it was hardly worth eating, so as they walked into the forest, Hansel scattered little pieces of his bread on to the path behind them.

They walked deeper into the forest than ever before and, once their parents had left them, the children felt utterly alone. At lunchtime, Gretel shared her piece of bread with her brother, and they fell asleep. When they awoke, the sky was quite dark, so Hansel took his sister by the hand and looked for the breadcrumb path by the light of the moon. If it were not for the great number of birds living in the forest, Hansel's plan would surely have worked, but the birds had eaten every crumb in sight. Now there was no way for Hansel and Gretel to find their way home.

The children walked all night, and all the next day, with no more than a few berries to eat. They began to worry that they might be lost forever. When they heard a pretty little bird singing, they stopped to listen. As it flew off, the two children followed until it landed on the roof of a small cottage. The hungry children went closer. To their surprise, the cottage was made entirely of sweets and cakes and breads of all sorts, with windows of clear spun sugar.

'We'll have a feast,' said Hansel, who broke off a piece of roof, while Gretel nibbled a window frame. While they filled their empty stomachs, a high-pitched voice interrupted their enjoyment, 'Who's that gnawing at my house? Is it a little mouse?'

Hansel and Gretel replied, 'It's only us,' and carried on eating, enjoying the cottage very much.

The door sprang open revealing an ugly, old woman leaning on a cane. 'Children!' she squealed. 'Come in, my dears, you must be very tired. Let me give you a place to rest.' Though they were alarmed by the woman's appearance, the children longed to have someone take care of them, so they followed her inside. They ate a delicious dinner and went to bed with their stomachs full. As they slept, the old woman chuckled, for she was not kind at all, but an evil witch.

Before the sun rose, the witch pulled Hansel from his bed and locked him in the stables where no one could hear him shout. To Gretel she said, 'Get out of bed and make your brother a big breakfast. When he's fat enough I'll eat him right up.' Gretel wept and wailed for her brother, but had to do as the witch told her. Her brother ate a hearty breakfast while she got nothing but scraps. Every day, the witch would visit young Hansel to see how much fatter he had become. 'Stretch out your finger, little boy,' she would order. Clever Hansel realized her eyesight was poor. Each day he stretched out a chicken bone instead of his finger, and the witch believed he was still as thin as ever.

Weeks went by, and the witch could no longer wait for the boy to get fat. She lit the oven and ordered Gretel to climb inside to check that it was hot enough. Realizing that the witch intended to cook her up first, Gretel said sweetly, 'But I don't know how to get in the oven.'

'Foolish child,' the witch scoffed, and stepped forward to show her. As soon as the witch's head and shoulders were through the oven door, Gretel gave her an enormous push and bolted it shut behind her, leaving the witch to roast.

Young Gretel ran to set her brother free, and the two were overjoyed to be together again. They decided to explore the witch's house before they left for home – and what a fortune they found! The witch had hidden boxes of all kinds of jewels and coins everywhere. The children took as much as they could carry and set off through the forest.

The longer they walked, the more familiar their surroundings became, until at last they spotted their house at the edge of the forest. When they saw their father in the doorway, they leapt towards him, weeping with joy. The woodcutter could hardly believe that Hansel and Gretel had returned to him. His wife had died, leaving him all alone, and he had been very unhappy without his children. Hansel and Gretel laid out all the jewels they had found at the witch's cottage, and laughed happily now that all their troubles were over.

The Elves And The Shoemaker

There was once a poor shoemaker, who had only enough leather left to make one pair of shoes. He had no money to buy more, so he cut out the pattern pieces for the shoes he wished to make, and put them aside until morning. The shoemaker lifted the candle stub he had been working by and trudged wearily up the stairs to the little rooms he shared with his wife above his workshop.

The next morning, the shoemaker opened the door to his workshop and gasped in surprise. There on the table was a fine pair of shoes, made from the leather he had left out. The shoemaker picked them up to take a closer look, and could not find a single fault. They were perfectly made. At that moment, the bell above the door of the workshop jingled and a customer walked in. She urgently needed a new pair of shoes, and when she saw the ones in the shoemaker's hands, knew she had found just the pair.

The shoes were sold in a flash, and with the money he had made the shoemaker bought enough leather to make two more pairs. He cut the pattern pieces out that evening and went up to bed for a good night's rest.

The next morning the shoemaker returned to his workshop feeling refreshed. He was ready to work, but the two pairs of shoes had already been made overnight. The shoemaker had nothing else to do but sell the beautiful shoes, and this was quickly done, leaving him enough money to buy leather for four pairs. Once more, the following morning, four pairs of ready-made shoes sat on his workshop counter. These strange events continued, until eventually the shoemaker was no longer poor, and customers came from far and wide to buy shoes from his workshop.

One night, just before Christmas, the shoemaker made up his mind to find out who had been helping him. He and his wife hid behind a curtain leading to the workshop area and waited. As the clock struck midnight, two little elves ran into the room wearing not even a scrap of clothing between them. They clambered on to the counter and set to work making shoes. The shoemaker was amazed at just how well the little elves stitched and hammered. He could not believe how quickly they completed all the work before they skipped off into the darkness.

The shoemaker's wife looked at him and said, 'We must show the elves how much we appreciate everything they have done for us. I will make them both a little outfit, with hats and jackets to keep them warm.' The shoemaker nodded in agreement and said,

'And I'll make a perfect little pair of shoes for them both.'

When the shoemaker and his wife had finished, they laid everything out on the workshop counter instead of any cut-out pattern pieces. They then hid behind the curtain again and waited to see what would happen.

As the clock struck twelve, the little elves ran in and discovered their brand new sets of clothes. They laughed and hugged each other in excitement. They dressed themselves, quick as a flash, and danced and skipped across the counter and out of the door. The elves were never to be seen again, but the shoemaker's business continued to be a great success, and he never worried about being poor again.

The Steadfast Tin Soldier

There was once a small boy who, on one particular birthday, was given a box of twenty-five tin soldiers. They all stood stiffly to attention in their smart uniforms, each with a rifle over his shoulder and a feather in his hat.

Each soldier looked exactly the same except for the one who had been made last. The tin had run out, leaving him with just one leg. He still stood as proudly to attention as each of his friends, and shouldered his rifle very well.

The boy set his tin soldiers out on the table along with his other toys. There was a castle with real windows so you could see inside, a miniature lake with trees around it, and a group of swans swimming across the water. In the door of the castle was a pretty paper ballerina wearing a gauze dress. Her leg was held up so far behind her that it could not be seen at all. The tin soldier assumed that just like him, she had only one leg. He decided that he should marry her, if she would have an ordinary soldier like him.

When it was time for the toys to all be put away, the tin
soldier hid behind the box where he would not be noticed,
and waited for the lights to be put out. From there he
could admire the ballerina all night. As soon as the family
were asleep, the other toys came to life and began to make
mischief with one another.

Only the tin soldier and the ballerina stayed still. From
across the table, she seemed to be holding out her arms to
the tin soldier. He steadfastly refused to take his eyes from
hers. At midnight the clock struck twelve and up popped
the lid of the jack-in-a-box. Out sprang an imp, who
skipped across the table. 'Stop your staring, tin soldier,' he
squealed. The tin soldier ignored him.

In the morning, the little boy came down to play, and
discovered the tin soldier near the castle. To keep it safe,
he placed the tin soldier on the windowsill, out of the way.
A sudden gust of wind sent the poor soldier flying out of
the window, and when the boy went to find him, he was
nowhere to be seen. The tin soldier could not make a fuss

while he was wearing his uniform. He stood stiffly to attention in the dirt at the side of the road, even when it began to rain and even when two naughty boys discovered him. 'Look! A tin soldier,' said one. 'Let's make him a ship.' So they made a little ship out of folded newspaper and set it in the gutter. As soon as they put the tin soldier into the ship, it was whirled about and whisked away by the current. Still the tin soldier stood to attention, even when a large water rat asked him where he thought he was going without permission.

'If only the pretty ballerina was with me,' the soldier thought to himself, 'I could stand almost anything.'

The poor tin soldier stood stiffly to attention as he sailed out of reach of the water rat. When the paper ship became so wet that he sank right through the bottom, he still behaved like a proper soldier. Floating around in the water, he looked like a rather tasty snack to the fish in those parts, and he was soon swallowed right up.

It was pitch black inside the fish, and the tin soldier did not know what to do. He was tossed and churned from side to side and up and down. At last the tin soldier glimpsed daylight again. The fish that had swallowed him had been caught and was being cut open on the kitchen counter of the very house he had been lost from. The cook cried out in astonishment, and plucked him from the fish's belly. She took him straight up to the playroom. Everyone was very impressed by the tin soldier's adventure – all except the tin soldier himself, who was rather humiliated that such a thing could have happened to him. There was the ballerina though, looking prettier than ever, and the tin soldier gazed at her adoringly. Just then, and for no reason at all, the little boy picked the soldier up in the tips of his fingers and tossed him into the fire.

The fire was horribly hot, but the tin soldier could still see the pretty ballerina, so he didn't mind. Then a sudden wind gusted through the playroom, and the ballerina was caught up and swept towards the flames. The paper ballerina quickly became a pile of ash, while the steadfast soldier made of tin melted into the shape of a devoted heart, and they were together forever.

Sleeping Beauty

A King and Queen, who had hoped for a child for many years, at last had a beautiful baby daughter. They planned a lavish christening and invited the seven fairies of the kingdom. Each fairy would bestow a wonderful gift on the Princess to give her the best qualities imaginable. They would all receive a casket of gold in thanks. Once the christening ceremony was complete, every guest joined the King, the Queen and the Princess at their palace for an enormous celebration feast. The table was set with the finest crystal goblets, golden plates and jewel-encrusted silverware. Everyone chattered excitedly to see it.

Suddenly there was a gasp – the whole hall quietened, turning to see what had caused such alarm. In the entrance was a small, wizened old fairy. Everyone had thought she was dead, so she hadn't been invited. The King hastily ordered an extra place for her, but as there was not an eighth casket of gold prepared for her, the fairy scowled in resentment.

Seated close by, a good fairy overheard
the miserable creature muttering her
indignation under her breath. She
decided to hang back as the others
lined up to present their gifts. She
cleverly hid herself behind a tapestry,
so that she would be certain to see
the Princess last.

The first fairy took her place in front of the
Princess's crib and gave her the gift of beauty. The
next gave her wit and laughter; the third, gracefulness.
The fourth fairy gave the gift of wonderful dancing. The
fifth chose that the Princess should sing like an angel, and
the sixth gave the gift of incredible musical talent.

While the good fairy remained hidden, the old fairy took
her place at the crib. With a venomous look at the King
and Queen, she announced, 'I give the Princess the gift of
a short life. She will prick her hand on a spindle and die.'

As the old fairy swept from the hall, everyone began
wailing and weeping. The good fairy was ready. She
revealed herself at once and said in a strong voice,
'I cannot undo what has been done. I can only help as best
I can. When the Princess pricks her hand she shall not die
– instead she shall fall into the deepest sleep imaginable.

Her sleep will last one hundred years, until a prince comes to awaken her with a kiss. This is my gift.'

So that the Princess could avoid such a terrible fate, a proclamation was made across the land that every spindle should be destroyed. For sixteen years the King, the Queen and the Princess lived joyful lives. The Princess did not so much as graze a knee or stub a toe as she grew, and never saw so much as a needle and thread, let alone a spindle. By and by, the King and Queen felt reassured that all would be well for their daughter, and they felt safe enough to leave her for a few days.

Having never been allowed to wander alone before, the excited Princess explored the palace. She climbed to the highest tower, where she came upon a tiny room in which an old servant sat at a spinning wheel and spindle. The servant knew nothing of the proclamation and didn't even know who the Princess was. She smiled and offered to show the Princess how the spindle worked. The Princess reached out, and, just as the old fairy had said, pricked her finger on its point. She slumped to the ground at once, and fell into the deepest sleep imaginable.

The old woman rushed for help, and the palace's servants tried all they could to awaken the Princess, but nothing worked. Returning to the palace, the King and Queen came upon such noise and chaos, they knew at once that something terrible had happened. Their daughter was carried to the finest room and laid on the most comfortable bed to be found.

The good fairy soon heard of the Princess's fate and rushed to the palace. Knowing that, a century later, the Princess would find herself among strangers, the fairy decided then and there that the whole palace should sleep until she awoke. A proclamation was sent out that no one should come near the palace, and as silence fell, a circle of trees rose up around it. Soon the palace could not be seen at all.

A hundred years passed by, and memories faded. One day a young Prince, hunting in the forest, rode by and spotted the palace's towers rising up through the trees. He asked who lived there. Some people thought that the tangle of trees hid a ruined castle, others that an ogre lived there. One man, having lived a long time, told the Prince the story of a beautiful Princess who slept in the palace beyond the trees. It was said that she was enchanted to sleep for a hundred years.

Being an adventurous young man, the Prince decided to explore. As he approached, the tangle of trees magically parted to allow him through. What he saw inside the palace almost stopped him in his tracks, for all around were the softly breathing statues of people and animals, frozen in a moment a century old. But the Prince was young and valiant; he strode forward in search of the Princess, crossing the courtyard and climbing the palace's grand staircase. By and by he came to a large chamber, garlanded with flowers. In the centre of it stood a bed, and on it lay a beautiful young Princess, sleeping peacefully. The Prince fell to his knees at her side and leant forward to kiss her. At his kiss the enchantment was lifted at last. The Princess's eyes fluttered open to see the handsome young Prince who had come for her. 'I'm so glad you have come,' she sighed.

The Prince and Princess fell instantly in love, and the servants, newly awakened, began to arrange a lavish wedding ceremony, to be held that evening. The whole palace rejoiced, and the feast was the most extraordinary the kingdom had ever seen. Though it had been a hundred years since they had played, the palace musicians put on a grand performance and everyone danced into the night.

Wild Swans

In a far away kingdom there lived a King, with his eleven charming sons and a beautiful daughter, named Elise. The Princess and her brothers were the happiest of children, but this was not to last. The King decided to remarry, and chose a cruel woman as his wife. The new Queen sent Elise far from home and told the King such lies about his sons that he could no longer even bear to look at them.

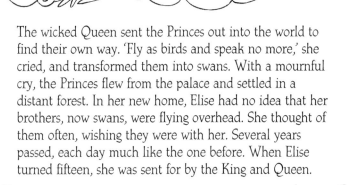

The wicked Queen sent the Princes out into the world to find their own way. 'Fly as birds and speak no more,' she cried, and transformed them into swans. With a mournful cry, the Princes flew from the palace and settled in a distant forest. In her new home, Elise had no idea that her brothers, now swans, were flying overhead. She thought of them often, wishing they were with her. Several years passed, each day much like the one before. When Elise turned fifteen, she was sent for by the King and Queen.

How her stepmother fumed when she saw how beautiful Elise had become! She longed to turn the girl into a bird as she had her brothers, but the King demanded to see his daughter. The Queen tried spell after spell to ruin the girl's looks, but none of them had any effect. Elise was just too kind and good. So the wicked woman rubbed a stinging juice into the Princess's skin and put an evil-smelling ointment on her hair. Elise was simply unrecognizable, and the King sent the girl away, sure that she wasn't his child.

Elise wandered the palace, searching for her brothers. When she realized they were no longer there, the poor girl walked and walked until she came to a forest. There she made a bed upon the mossy ground and fell asleep.

The next day, Elise went deeper into the forest, where she found a lake. Its surface was as shiny as a mirror. Elise saw how dreadful she looked, so she washed and washed until she looked like a princess again. Now very hungry, Elise met an old woman who kindly offered her food. Elise asked the woman if she had seen her brothers, but she replied, 'I have not, but I did see eleven lovely swans on the river.'

Elise thanked her and started out along the riverbank, searching for any sign of the swans. At the ocean, where she could go no further, Elise spotted eleven gleaming white feathers floating in the breaking surf, and silhouetted in the setting sun eleven swans were flying in to land.

As the sun dipped below the horizon, the swans gathered around Elise. Their feathers vanished, revealing her missing brothers. The Princes were so happy to see Elise they could not stop hugging her as they explained.

'We fly as swans,' said one.

'Only during the day,' the youngest exclaimed. 'At night we are human again.'

'Yes, and we must reach land before the sun sets,' added the first, 'or we'll tumble into the ocean and drown.'

Elise learnt that the brothers could fly home just once a year. They had only one resting place on the way – a small rock in the ocean. Now they had found her, there were just two days left before the brothers must leave. They decided that Elise should return with them, so the Princes set to weaving a mat of rushes on which they could carry her. As the sun rose on their final day, the swans took the mat in their bills with Elise still sleeping between them.

As they flew, the youngest Prince shaded Elise from the sun with his wings. When they reached the little rock in the ocean, they spent the night huddled close together.

The following day's journey took Elise and the swans over many lands, with breathtaking sights of strange mountains and fairy palaces, where humans were forbidden. At last, the swans descended towards the cave where they lived.

That night, the Princess dreamt that she met a beautiful young fairy. The fairy looked so much like the old woman from the forest that they could only be one and the same. The fairy whispered, 'You can break the spell on your brothers, Elise. Be brave and determined. Gather stinging nettles from the churchyard nearby – take as many as you can, no matter how much they burn your hands. Tear them up until they turn to flax, then weave coats for your brothers. They will be transformed into men once more. But, from this moment until the task is complete, you may not utter another word, or you will fail and your brothers will die.'

When she awoke, Elise began her task in earnest. She gathered nettles and bruised them into flax, and spun and wove the first of the magical green coats. The Princes flew home that night to discover their sister struck dumb – she would not speak a word. When the youngest saw what she

was doing, and how her hands and arms blistered, he wept. Drenched in his tears, Elise's skin was healed, and her pain vanished, but she still refused to speak.

The next day, Elise heard the sound of a hunt approaching and quickly hid her work. The leader of the hunting party, the King of this land, thought that he had never seen anyone more lovely. He asked Elise how she came to be there, but of course she could not reply.

The King would not leave her alone in the forest and when Elise said nothing he swept her up on his horse and took her back to his castle. There the Princess was dressed in fine robes and the King declared that he would marry her the next day, though she still hadn't spoken a word. Elise

was shown to a bedchamber. She smiled for the first time in hours — everything from the forest had been brought to the castle, including the nettle coat she had made.

The King made plans for the wedding, all the while ignoring his bishop's hints that Elise might be a witch. During the ceremony, the King did not notice as the bishop pressed the crown down viciously on Elise's head, and she still did not utter a word because it would harm her brothers. If only she could explain to the King, who she had grown to love, why she could not speak.

Still, each night, Elise wove coats for her brothers. One night, when the flax ran out, she crept from the castle to the churchyard for more nettles. Who should be awake at night to see her? None other than the suspicious bishop. Now he knew he was right — she was a witch. He went to the King to inform him. Tears formed in the King's eyes at the news, but he too grew suspicious.

Elise noticed the King's mood darken, but did not know why. She continued her task with determination. With just one magical coat left to complete, she went out to collect more nettles one last time. Little did Elise know that the King and the bishop followed close behind. When they saw her plucking nettles from the churchyard at night, the King knew she must be condemned as a witch.

Sent to the castle dungeons with nothing but her woven coats and nettles, Elise carried on with her task, unable to think of anything else. As the evening drew on, the young Queen heard the sound of wings at the high window of her cell and looked up with delight to see the youngest of her swan brothers. They had found her.

This was her final night to complete the last of the coats, so Elise did not stop. Mice brought the nettles closer, and a song thrush sang all night to help her work. The Princes stood at the castle gates and demanded an audience with the King, but when the sun rose they were nowhere to be seen – though eleven swans flew mournfully overhead.

As the cart pulled Elise towards her execution, she wove constantly, trying to finish the final coat for her brothers before her death. A crowd gathered and jeered as she sat weaving what they thought must be spells. Before the angry people could take the coats from her, Elise threw them into the air as her eleven swan brothers swooped above. As each of them was covered by a coat, they transformed back into men, all except the youngest, whose coat was not quite complete. The unfinished sleeve of his coat meant that one of his arms would forever remain a swan's wing. Elise sank to the floor with relief as her brothers gathered round her.

'At last I can speak,' she said. 'I am no witch.' The Princes loudly agreed, and told the King of the events that had led to this moment. As they spoke, flowers bloomed, church bells pealed and song thrushes added their music. The King and Elise could not have been happier.

Rapunzel

A man and a woman had lived happily together for many years, but always longed for a child. One day, it seemed their wishes might be granted – a baby was on the way.

Near their little house was a wonderful garden, full of trees and glorious flowers, surrounded by a high wall. From her window the woman could see over the wall into the garden, where dozens of delicious rampion plants grew. She longed to taste some. However, she knew that no one must ever go into the garden, as it belonged to a terrible enchantress.

The woman grew sad and restless, and her worried husband asked, 'What's the matter, my darling wife?'

'If only I could eat some rampion, from the garden behind our house, I would feel so much better,' she replied.

The man loved his wife so dearly that he decided to do whatever he could to get her what she desired. That evening, he crept over the garden's high wall and pulled up some of the plants for her. But once his wife had tasted the delicious rampion, she longed for it more than ever. The woman's husband knew he would not get a moment's

peace unless he got her more. The next evening he crept into the garden again but, to his horror, the terrible enchantress was waiting for him.

'How dare you enter my garden and steal from me?' she screeched. 'I shall make you pay for this.'

'Oh, please let me go,' the man begged. 'I really only took the rampion because my wife longed for it so.'

The enchantress looked thoughtfully at the man and then said, 'In that case, take as much as you can carry, but on one condition. As soon as your child is born, you must give it to me, and I shall care for it like a mother.' Too terrified to disagree, the man accepted this condition and left, his arms full of delicious rampion.

As she had promised, the instant the baby was born, the enchantress appeared. She lifted the little girl into her arms, naming her Rapunzel, and took her away.

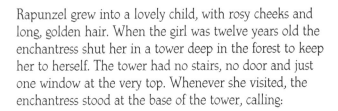

Rapunzel grew into a lovely child, with rosy cheeks and long, golden hair. When the girl was twelve years old the enchantress shut her in a tower deep in the forest to keep her to herself. The tower had no stairs, no door and just one window at the very top. Whenever she visited, the enchantress stood at the base of the tower, calling:

> 'Rapunzel, Rapunzel,
> Let down your golden hair.'

Rapunzel's hair, like gold spun into the finest thread, was as long as the tower was tall. When the enchantress called, Rapunzel unwound her braid, and let it drop out of the window to the ground. Up the enchantress would climb.

Rapunzel lived like this for three long years, all alone in the tower. She filled her days with music, making the forest echo with her favourite songs. One day, a young Prince riding through the forest passed near the tower. He heard such lovely singing that he slowed his horse so that he could listen. The Prince longed to meet the owner of such a voice, but he could see no way to enter the tower and rode home disappointed. Unable to forget Rapunzel's voice, the Prince rode out every day to listen to her sing.

One day, as he stood listening, the Prince saw the old enchantress arrive at the tower. He heard her call out:

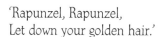

'Rapunzel, Rapunzel,
Let down your golden hair.'

He watched as a long braid fell down, and the enchantress climbed up. The Prince, delighted to discover the way into the tower, returned at twilight the next day and called out:

'Rapunzel, Rapunzel,
Let down your golden hair.'

At once the braid fell at his feet, and the Prince climbed it. When he appeared at the tower's window, Rapunzel was a little afraid at first, having never met anyone other than the enchantress before. However, when the Prince spoke of how much he loved hearing her sing, and how he had longed to meet her, she was moved. The Prince visited often and soon asked if she would marry him. Seeing that he was both handsome and kind-hearted, Rapunzel knew that he would be far sweeter to her than the enchantress could ever be. Taking his hand, she said simply, 'Yes.' However, knowing how impossible it would be to escape, Rapunzel added, 'I will marry you, but I cannot leave unless you fetch a skein of silk each time you visit. I'll turn the silk into a knotted ladder, climb down and come away with you.'

Until the ladder could be made, they decided that the Prince would visit each evening in secret, as the enchantress came during the day. The arrangement worked well, and the ladder was almost complete, but one day Rapunzel forgot herself. She asked the enchantress, 'How is it that you weigh so much more than the Prince who visits me?'

The enchantress turned on her furiously, 'You wicked girl. This tower was to keep you far away from everyone, but you have been lying to me.' Taking a pair of scissors, the enchantress grasped Rapunzel's hair, and hacked at

the braid until it fell to the floor. She took Rapunzel away and abandoned her in a barren wasteland. The enchantress returned to the tower to lie in wait for the Prince. When he called for Rapunzel she dropped the end of the girl's braid to the ground for the Prince to climb up. When he appeared at the window, the wicked enchantress glared at him with furious eyes. 'Ha!' she cackled. 'You've come to find your true love, but you will never see Rapunzel again.' Without thinking, the Prince leapt from the window to the ground. Thorny bushes broke his fall, and saved his life, but the long thorns tore into his eyes, and made him blind.

For months and years the Prince wandered among the trees of the forest, guided by nothing but the touch of his fingertips. He ate just roots and berries, and every day he wept over the loss of Rapunzel. This was all the Prince could do, until one day he reached a barren land.

He came to a cottage, where a young woman and her twin children lived in poverty. He heard a voice so familiar, that he could not help but stumble towards it. Rapunzel! She was so astonished to see her Prince that she pulled him into her arms, weeping with joy. A precious tear fell into each of the Prince's eyes, and in a moment his sight was restored. Reunited with Rapunzel, and seeing his children for the very first time, the Prince was overjoyed. He led them all back to his kingdom, where they lived long and happy lives.

Cinderella

There was once a gentleman whose wife had died, leaving him with their young daughter to raise. He worried that she would not have a mother as she grew up, and decided to marry again. The woman he chose had two daughters of her own, and he felt sure they would all get on well.

Once the wedding was over, the woman and her daughters moved into the house. They took the best rooms for themselves, and the woman sent her stepdaughter to work in the kitchens. The girl cleaned and scrubbed, swept and brushed, and at night she slept on a straw bed. When her work was finished, she would go to the chimney corner to rest, which earned her the nickname 'Cinderella'.

When the King's son decided to throw a ball, Cinderella longed to be invited. The most fashionable people were going, and her stepsisters constantly talked about what they might wear. Poor Cinderella was far more beautiful than them both, but the only clothes she had were tatty rags, which would never do. Her stepsisters teased her endlessly, and laughed at the thought of their little stepsister going to a ball.

The day of the ball arrived, and the sisters fussed and preened until they were satisfied with their outfits. Cinderella helped them decorate their hair. As their carriage pulled away from the house that evening, she sighed sadly to herself, 'If only I could go to the ball as well.'

Her godmother, who happened to be a fairy, overheard Cinderella's words. She decided that the girl had as much right to go to the ball as her stepsisters. 'Dry your eyes, dear Cinderella,' she said. 'You can still go to the ball. If you fetch me a nice round pumpkin from the garden, I will show you how,' said her godmother, smiling happily.

Cinderella went straight to the pumpkin patch and fetched the best-looking pumpkin she could find. She watched as

her godmother hollowed it out. Cinderella gasped when
the fairy tapped the pumpkin with her wand. The
pumpkin was transformed into a splendid golden carriage.

Her godmother then sent Cinderella to fetch six mice from
the kitchen. These she transformed into a team of
handsome mouse-coloured horses. Now they needed a
coachman to drive the horses, so Cinderella fetched the rat
trap. Her godmother picked out the smartest-looking rat
and tapped him with her wand. The rat turned instantly
into a charming coachman, who took charge of the horses.

Any fine carriage is not complete without footmen, so
Cinderella ran into the garden again and selected six
lizards that were basking in the evening sunshine. Her
godmother transformed them into six handsome footmen,
who jumped up to stand at the back of the carriage.

'It's wonderful!' cried Cinderella, 'But what am I to wear?'

Cinderella's godmother looked at her outfit and shook her
head. She closed her eyes and tapped the girl gently on top

of her head, transforming her completely. Her hair bounced up into pretty curls, with ribbons wound through it. Her tatty clothes became a glittering ball gown, and her practical shoes became the most delicate glass slippers anyone had ever seen.

'Be warned, Cinderella,' her godmother said gravely. 'You must promise to leave the ball by midnight. The moment the clock strikes twelve, your dress and your carriage will return to their original forms.' Cinderella made her promise and stepped into the carriage. The horses trotted off merrily, with the coachman whistling and the footmen standing proudly to attention.

Cinderella made a very grand entrance at the ball. People whispered, and the Prince soon heard that a beautiful princess had arrived. He could not resist going to greet her and was astonished at how lovely she looked. He led

Cinderella through to the dance floor and whirled her around and around to the music. Even her stepsisters admired the beautiful stranger, but they did not realize who it was. The Prince spent the whole evening dancing only with Cinderella, and could not take his eyes off her. Just when she thought she couldn't be any happier, Cinderella heard the clock strike the quarter before midnight. She quickly made her excuses and left, remembering the promise to her godmother.

When her stepsisters arrived home, Cinderella was in her normal clothes, and innocently asked, 'Did you enjoy the ball?' The two girls gushed excitedly about the princess who had been at the ball, and talked at length about how much attention the Prince had given her. The Prince was to throw another ball the following night in order to see the mysterious princess again.

The next night, Cinderella begged her godmother to help her once more. She wore even finer clothes than before. She danced and danced with the Prince, and quite forgot the time. When the clock struck twelve, she ran out so quickly that one of her slippers was left behind. The Prince rushed after her, but when he asked the guards if they had seen a princess pass they replied that they had only seen a scruffy-looking maid.

When her stepsisters came home, they told Cinderella how the princess had rushed out of the ball so quickly that she had left a slipper behind. They were certain the Prince was in love with her. A few days later, the Prince announced that he would gladly marry the girl whose foot fit the glass slipper. He ordered that every woman in the land should try it on until the princess was found.

The courtiers arrived at Cinderella's house to great fanfare. Her stepsisters desperately tried to wedge their feet into the glass slipper that was held out for them, but their feet were just too big. When Cinderella timidly suggested that she should like to try it on, they laughed and laughed. However, the courtiers were obedient servants and insisted that Cinderella get her chance as the Prince had ordered. Her foot fitted into the slipper like a hand into a glove. When she produced the matching shoe there could be no doubt about her identity. Her stepsisters were astounded.

Cinderella's godmother appeared, and transformed her once more into the dazzling stranger from the ball. She went to meet the Prince, and he asked for her hand in marriage at once. Kind Cinderella begged him to allow her sisters to live at court as well, and they soon found husbands of their own.

The Princess And The Pea

Long ago, there was a Prince who wished more than anything to marry a true princess and bring her home to his parents, the King and Queen. He looked everywhere for the perfect bride, but no matter how many princesses he met, the Prince knew there was something lacking in each of them. He returned home alone, feeling quite sad.

Several nights after his return, a terrible storm blew up, rattling the palace windows with thunder and lightning and covering the world in darkness. An urgent knocking at the door startled everyone, and the King himself went to find out who could be outside on such an awful night.

A girl stood at the door, soaked to the skin. She asked if she might have a bed for the night, as she was so far from home. The girl claimed to be a true Princess, but it was impossible to tell from her appearance.

The Prince's mother, the Queen, narrowed her eyes. She thought to herself, 'I'll soon find this one out,' and slipped away to

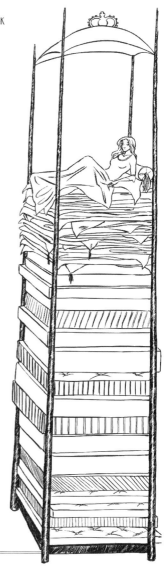

help prepare a bed for their guest.
The bed was stripped of its covers
and its mattress, and at the base
she placed three small, hard peas.
Then twenty mattresses were piled
over them, followed by twenty of
the palace's softest feather quilts.

The following day, the girl was
asked how well she had slept, and
replied, 'Quite awfully, in fact.
There were hard lumps in my bed,
and I've not had a wink of sleep.
I tossed and turned all night, and
now I'm covered in bruises!'

The Queen listened intently.
Clearly the girl was a true Princess,
for who else would be able to feel
three tiny peas through so many
mattresses and quilts? Only a true
Princess could be so sensitive.

This was surely the perfect bride for
the King's son, and the two became
husband and wife as soon as the
arrangements could be made.

Snow White

Long ago and deep in winter, a Queen sat at her window sewing and daydreaming. As she gazed at the falling snow, the Queen pricked her finger, and three drops of blood fell to the ground. 'If I only had a child,' she sighed, looking at the drops of blood. 'Her skin might be as white as snow, her lips as red as blood and her hair as dark as the night sky. I would be so happy.' Sure enough, some time later she had a baby girl, named Snow White, but sadly the Queen died soon after.

A year later Snow White's father remarried. The new Queen was beautiful, but proud of her looks. If she suspected that anyone was prettier than her, she rushed to her magical mirror and asked, 'Mirror, mirror, on the wall, who in this kingdom is fairest of all?' The mirror reassured her each time, 'My Queen, you are fairest of all.' The Queen would be soothed at these words, for she knew the mirror could only speak the truth.

It was not until Snow White was twelve years old that the mirror gave the Queen a most unexpected response. 'My Queen, you are more fair than all who are here, but fairer still is Snow White, I fear.' The Queen was outraged, and turned a very particular shade of green. Snow White was indeed growing more beautiful each day.

The Queen's pride turned to envy, and in the following years each time she saw Snow White she hated her more. So one day she sent the girl out into the forest with a huntsman who was to kill her and bring back her heart as evidence. The huntsman was loyal, but he could not bring himself to kill Snow White. He took back the heart of a wild boar instead, and let Snow White go in the forest.

All alone, Snow White ran through the forest. As night fell she came to a cottage, and went inside. She found seven tiny beds in a row and a small table, with a meal set out. Snow White ate a little from each plate and drank a little from each cup. She did not want to leave one person with nothing at all. Then, after trying out each bed, she fell into a deep sleep on the one which was most comfortable.

While she slept, the seven dwarves who lived in the cottage came home. They saw at once that someone had visited. The first dwarf asked, 'Who has sat in my chair?'

'And who has eaten from my plate?' wondered the second.

'Who has eaten some of my vegetables?' said the third.

'Who has taken some of my bread?' wondered the fourth.

'Who has used my knife?' asked the fifth, crossly.

'And who has used my fork?' said the sixth.

'Who has drunk from my cup?' the seventh dwarf puzzled.

Each worried dwarf noticed a dent in his bed, except the seventh, who saw not a dent – but Snow White herself. The dwarves held up their candles to see. 'What a beautiful girl,'

they whispered. They were so relieved that the seventh dwarf did not mind being put out of his bed for the night.

When she awoke, Snow White was alarmed to see the dwarves, but when she explained how she came to be there they were very kind. The dwarves let her stay, and each morning as they left to mine for gold, they told Snow White to take care, in case the Queen discovered she lived.

The Queen, meanwhile, thought she must once more be the most beautiful woman in the kingdom. She gazed into her mirror and asked, 'Mirror, mirror, on the wall, who in this kingdom is fairest of all?' The truthful mirror replied, 'My Queen, you are the fairest of all in sight, but in the forest with the dwarves this night, there is none lovelier than Snow White.' The Queen was horrified. Snow White was still alive. Her heart was filled with envy once more, so she made a plan to get rid of the girl once and for all.

The next day, the Queen dressed as an old pedlar woman and went to the forest in search of the dwarves' cottage. 'Pretty things, pretty things,' she cried. Snow White could not resist and excitedly asked, 'What have you to sell?'

'Every colour of stay lace, my dear,' said the woman. 'Let me re-lace your dress for you.' The woman had a pretty set of laces for Snow White's dress, but pulled them so tightly the poor girl gasped for air. She went pale and fell to the floor. Satisfied that the girl was dead, the Queen ran off.

When the dwarves found Snow White, they saw at once that her dress was laced so tightly that she couldn't breathe. They quickly cut the laces and again warned her to take care when she was alone. They knew the old pedlar woman could only have been the Queen in disguise.

The Queen, meanwhile, gazed into her mirror and asked, 'Mirror, mirror, on the wall, who in this kingdom is fairest of all?' The mirror said truthfully, 'My Queen, you are the fairest of all in sight, but in the forest with the dwarves this night, there is none lovelier than Snow White.' The woman was furious, and made a plan much worse than the last. Using her magical powers, the wicked Queen created a poisoned comb, and in disguise she took it to the cottage.

'Pretty things, pretty things,' she cried out again.

'I cannot let you in,' said Snow White, gazing at the comb.

'Just let me comb your hair for you then,' suggested the woman. Snow White allowed it and, as the poison took hold, fell to the floor, surely dead. The dwarves were horrified to find Snow White lying on the ground once more, but suspected the Queen immediately. One took the comb from Snow White's hair, and she stirred at once and told them what had happened. Again they warned their friend to take care when she was alone.

The Queen, convinced she had triumphed over Snow White at last, again asked, 'Mirror, mirror, on the wall, who in this kingdom is fairest of all?' Once more, the mirror could only reply, 'My Queen, you are the fairest of all in sight, but in the forest with the dwarves this night, there is none lovelier than Snow White.' At this, the Queen flew into a rage and swore that she would find a way to kill Snow White.

So the Queen took the sweetest-looking apple she could find – rosy red on one side, pearly white on the other – and, with her most horrible spell, made one side of it as poisonous as possible. She disguised herself a third time and went once more to knock at the door of the cottage. 'I can't let you in!' cried Snow White. 'But surely, you could just have one of these delicious apples? Here, take this one,' the woman smiled, as sweetly as she could. 'We can share it.' She then cut the apple in two and passed half to Snow White. Seeing the woman eating happily, the girl felt reassured and took a bite. But the instant her lips touched her half of the apple, Snow White fell to the floor – dead.

'The dwarves won't help her now,' the Queen cackled to herself and ran to the castle to ask, 'Mirror, mirror, on the wall, who in this kingdom is fairest of all?' Its reply was music to her ears, 'My Queen, you are the fairest of all.'

The poor dwarves returned to their cottage that night to find their friend quite dead. Nothing they did would revive her, and they could do nothing but cry for three long days. The dwarves could not think of burying her in the cold, dark ground, so they built Snow White a beautiful glass coffin – her name engraved in golden letters upon it – and set it high on the mountain where they could always watch it.

Snow White lay in the coffin for many days, but her cheeks remained a rosy pink and her lips ruby red. She looked as though she was sleeping, but she still did not stir. All the animals of the forest came to visit, and one day a King's son, riding through the forest, came upon them. The instant he saw Snow White the Prince fell in love. He begged the dwarves to let him take Snow White to his palace, where she could be admired by everyone. The reluctant dwarves agreed, and the Prince's servants lifted Snow White up to carry her down the mountain.

As the sad procession moved off, one of the servants
stumbled over a tree root. The sudden movement caused a
small piece of apple, lodged in Snow White's throat, to fall
out. To everyone's surprise she suddenly awoke. The Prince
was so delighted he asked Snow White to marry him, and
the happy couple began planning a wonderful ceremony.

In the castle, the Queen once again asked, 'Mirror, mirror,
on the wall, who in this kingdom is fairest of all?' To her
horror it replied, 'My Queen, you are fairest of all in sight,
but the young Queen Snow White is fairest of all this
night.' The Queen uttered a curse so very vile that the
castle shook around her, and she fell down dead.

Twelve Dancing Princesses

There was once a King who had twelve lovely daughters. They slept in twelve beds all in one room, and when they went to bed the door was shut and locked behind them. However, each morning their shoes were found to be quite worn through, as though the Princesses had danced all night long. Nobody could understand how this happened.

The King made it known that if anyone could discover the secret, he would be allowed to choose one of the Princesses to marry, and would become the next King. However, any man who tried had only three days and nights to succeed. If he failed, he would be put to death.

One after another, princes from near and far came to the kingdom to try their luck. None of them succeeded, and the King feared that he would never discover where his daughters went each night.

At that time, an injured soldier returned to the kingdom. He met an old woman on the road, who told him of the

dancing Princesses. The soldier thought aloud, 'I should like to see if *I* can discover their secret.'

'Make sure you do not drink any of the wine the Princesses offer you,' the old woman warned. 'You must pretend to fall asleep and then put on this cloak,' she said, giving him a shimmering piece of fabric. 'It will make you invisible so that you can easily follow them.' The soldier took it gratefully and set off for the palace.

When the soldier arrived, he was welcomed as even the greatest prince had been. The King made sure that he was given fine clothes to wear, and he was shown to a bedchamber by the Princesses' room. From there, he could listen out for when they left and hopefully follow them.

That evening, the King's eldest daughter brought the soldier some wine to drink. He thanked her politely, but tipped it away when she wasn't looking. To make sure they believed he was sleeping, the soldier started snoring loudly. The Princesses giggled softly as they got ready for the night ahead. However, the youngest Princess was worried and frowned. 'Perhaps we shouldn't go tonight?' she wondered.

'Nonsense,' her sisters scoffed. Then the eldest stood at the side of her bed, clapped her hands, and stood back. The bed sank down and a trapdoor opened, revealing a staircase below. She led the way, with her sisters following behind all in beautiful ball gowns and fresh dancing shoes.

The soldier, who had heard the noise of the trapdoor opening, covered himself with the cloak and tiptoed after them. He was so anxious to keep up with the Princesses, that he caught the hem of the youngest girl's dress, and she almost fell. 'Someone is here,' she cried.

'Nonsense,' her sisters scoffed, as they walked through an orchard of sparkling silver trees. The soldier snapped off a branch to take as proof of the night's events, and the youngest girl jumped at the noise. 'What was that?'

Her oldest sister reassured her, 'It is just our dancing partners, the Princes, asking us to hurry.'

Next they came to an orchard where the trees glimmered

with golden leaves, and another where they glittered and sparkled like diamonds. The soldier snapped a branch from a tree in each orchard, startling the youngest Princess again and again.

At last they came to the edge of a large lake, where twelve Princes were waiting in twelve little boats to row them all across the lake. The soldier stepped carefully into a boat with the youngest Princess, and they were rowed slowly, but surely, across the water.

When they reached the other side of the lake the Prince was more tired than usual, because of the extra weight, and very relieved to stop rowing. The youngest Princess stepped delicately out of the boat and smoothed down her gown. In the distance, her sisters were already heading towards the castle with its pretty turrets and the sound of music playing. She hurried to catch up, and the soldier quickly stepped out of the boat and followed behind her.

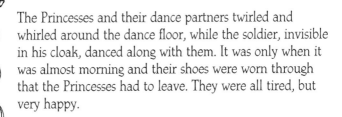

The Princesses and their dance partners twirled and whirled around the dance floor, while the soldier, invisible in his cloak, danced along with them. It was only when it was almost morning and their shoes were worn through that the Princesses had to leave. They were all tired, but very happy.

The Princes escorted them back to the edge of the lake and rowed them to the opposite shore. The soldier stepped into the boat of the eldest Princess this time, so that he would not alarm the youngest Princess again. When they reached the shore, everyone said good night, and promised to see each other again the very next evening.

Now that he knew their secret, the soldier ran on ahead of the twelve sisters. He rushed up the staircase as quietly as he could, and laid down on the bed in the next room and pretended to be asleep.

The Princesses smiled to hear him snoring, and everyone reassured their youngest sister saying, 'See, all went just as it should. You musn't worry so.' Each girl then took off her worn out shoes and hung up her ball gown, before falling into bed, exhausted.

The next day, the soldier decided that he would say nothing yet to the King about the Princesses' dancing.

He still had two more nights to discover more about their adventures. So he followed them again that evening, and again the next. Each night he came away with another memento from the magical world underground, and hid them all safely under his bed where the Princesses would not look.

After the soldier had spent three days and three nights at the palace, the King summoned him and said, 'Well, what have you discovered? Where do my daughters go each night? How do they wear out so many pairs of shoes?'

The Princesses stood waiting, sad that the soldier would die because he had failed to discover their secret. He stepped forward, cleared his throat so that everyone would hear him, and said, 'They spend each night dancing with twelve Princes in a magical world under the ground.'

The Princesses gasped in astonishment, and when the soldier showed the King the proof he had gathered, the youngest began to cry. The King asked his daughters if what the soldier said was true, and they had no choice but to be honest at last. So the soldier was allowed to choose one of the Princesses to marry, as he had been promised. He asked the eldest Princess to be his wife, and they were married the very next day.

The Little Mermaid

Deep in the world of the Ocean King lay a palace of coral
and shell. The King had six lovely daughters, who had
been looked after by their grandmother since the Queen
had died. She took great pride in taking good care of the
Princesses, especially the youngest, who was the loveliest of
them all. Like each of her sisters the youngest Princess had
the tail of a fish. Together they swam in and out of the
castle and gardens, playing with the fish that lived there.
When the sun shone above the surface of the sea, the light
played over their watery home, turning it all the colours of
the rainbow.

Each Princess had her own garden plot to take care of, and
the youngest took great delight in the pretty flowers she
grew. Most of all, she loved a statue of a boy, which had
fallen from the wreck of a ship. She liked nothing better
than to hear about the world he had come from, so her
grandmother told her everything she knew of the people
and places above the ocean. The Little Mermaid could not
wait until she was fifteen, when she would be allowed to
visit the surface to see this magical place for herself.

Each time one of the Little Mermaid's older sisters reached
the age of fifteen, she would come back from the surface
with tales of all she had seen. The first told stories of

bathing in the moonlight and the lights of a nearby city. The second talked of nothing but the glory of the setting sun. The third, who was braver, described how she had swum up a river and discovered castles and palaces and human children playing. The fourth was shy, and did not stray from the middle of the ocean, but it was beautiful enough for her. It was the depths of winter when the fifth Princess turned fifteen. She described the surface of the ocean covered in huge icebergs – she had climbed up on one to see great ships sailing by. All the while the Little Mermaid grew more and more impatient for her turn.

The Princesses who had seen above the ocean grew quite used to it, and much preferred to stay at home. They would only swim up if a storm was coming, and sing a warning to passing ships. Sadly, the sailors didn't recognize the singing of mermaids, and ignored their warnings.

When at last she reached her fifteenth birthday, the Little Mermaid eagerly headed for the surface. The sun was just setting, and the air was still. Close by, a ship lay at anchor, waiting for the wind to pick up. On board was a Prince, celebrating his sixteenth birthday. He was very handsome and the Little Mermaid swam closer to see him better. The crew set off a huge burst of fireworks in his honour at that very moment. The Little Mermaid was so startled by the noise that she dove down below the waves, emerging only to see the last cascades of light falling to the water below. The Prince stood on deck, gazing in wonder at the display, and the Little Mermaid was captivated by him. Although the hour was late, and the ocean was getting rougher, the Little Mermaid lingered, admiring the Prince from a distance.

The longer she stayed, the worse the weather became. Soon the sailors were struggling to control the ship in the stormy conditions. The grinding and creaking of timbers pulling in all directions became deafening, and with a loud crack the main mast broke in two, and crashed through the deck. Everyone on board was thrown into the waves. The Little Mermaid searched desperately for the Prince. She realized that he would not be able to breathe under water as she could. At last she found him, and all through the night she held his head above water, but his eyes remained closed. He looked so much like the statue in her palace garden that the Little Mermaid kissed his cheek, hoping he would wake. As the sun peeped above the horizon, she swam the Prince to shore and laid him carefully on the sand.

The Little Mermaid watched from the water as a beautiful young girl walking on the shore found the Prince. She could have been the Little Mermaid's twin. The girl ran for help, and the Little Mermaid watched as the Prince awoke and smiled at those around him. Then she waited for him to look back at the ocean and smile at her – he didn't, believing that the young girl on the shore had saved his life. Broken-hearted, the Little Mermaid swam home.

When the Little Mermaid told her sisters what she had seen above the surface, they decided to find out where the Prince lived so that their sister might see him again. The Little Mermaid visited every week, observing the Prince as closely as she dared, and wishing that she was human, too. The more she saw of the Prince, the more she wanted to learn about his world, but her grandmother had a stern warning. 'Be careful, little one,' she said. 'The world of humans is not for us. They have such short lives, and if you became human you would never be able to return to your ocean home.'

The Little Mermaid pestered her grandmother constantly, to tell her how she could become human. When at last her

grandmother revealed the secret, the Little Mermaid went bravely to ask the Sea Witch for help. The Sea Witch also offered a stern warning. 'It is not enough simply to become human,' she hissed. 'If you do, the Prince must also fall in love with you. If he marries anyone but you, your heart will shatter by the time the sun rises. You will return to the sea as nothing more than the drops of spray in the breaking surf. Do you understand?'

'I do,' whispered the Little Mermaid, too terrified of the Sea Witch to disagree.

'Very well,' the witch hissed, 'I will give you a potion. Drink it when you are close to shore, so that you can reach land safely. You will exchange your tail for human legs. But be warned – every step you take will be as painful as if you were walking on knives. In payment, I require only your beautiful voice – you will never be able to sing again.'

The Little Mermaid swallowed her fear, and took the potion, thanking the Sea Witch. She swam to the shore near the Prince's palace before she changed her mind. She drank the potion in one gulp. That instant her tail disappeared, and the Little Mermaid wiggled her newly formed toes, feeling for the sand beneath them. The moment she stood up, an astonishing pain shot through her feet. She would have cried out, but her voice had also gone. Carefully, she stepped out of the water just as the Prince was walking along the shore.

The Prince thought he had never seen anyone more beautiful. 'What is your name, girl?' he demanded. When the Little Mermaid didn't reply he asked, 'Where did you come from?' Her silence puzzled him. The Prince thought it best that he take the strange girl back to the palace, so that she could be looked after. There the Little Mermaid was dressed in the finest silks, and given a room of her own to sleep in. 'You remind me of a girl who once saved my life. You could be her twin,' he told her. 'She is the most beautiful girl in the world, and I would marry her tomorrow if I could.'

Even though the Little Mermaid could not speak, the Prince found that he enjoyed her company more than anyone else's, and kept her with him constantly. The Little Mermaid did not mind, for as long as she was near him, there was a chance that the Prince might fall in love with her instead of the girl from the beach. Each night the sad girl slipped quietly out of the palace and down to the shore to bathe her feet. Her mermaid sisters came to her there and gathered around her in the water, wishing she would speak to them, but she could not.

The Little Mermaid loved the Prince more and more each day that she spent with him. So on the day that the King

and Queen arranged for him to marry the girl he loved, she thought her heart was already broken. She sat through the wedding and the merry dancing afterwards, then went to the sea to wait for the sunrise. Her mermaid sisters gathered sadly around her. They had been to ask the Sea Witch for help, but there was only one solution. If the Little Mermaid could bring herself to kill the Prince before sunrise, she could return to the sea once more. But she just could not do it. She fell into the water as the red light spilled on to the horizon, and joined the drops of spray in the breaking surf.

When the Little Mermaid opened her eyes, she was surrounded by a crowd of beautiful, transparent creatures. They floated around her, smiling in welcome. To her surprise, when she looked down at herself, the Little Mermaid saw that she looked just like them.

'Welcome, Little Mermaid,' sang the beings around her, as she floated up and up into the sky with them. 'We are the daughters of the air, and you are now one of us.' As she looked back at the world she was leaving behind, the Little Mermaid spotted the Prince and his new wife walking along the shore. She was so happy in her new life, however, that her heart felt light at the sight of them. She knew she would be happier than she could ever have been before. And so she spent the rest of her days, carrying health and happiness around the world.

The Tinderbox

A soldier returning from battle met an old witch on the road home. She stopped him, saying, 'You look like a fine fellow. Great riches will come to you, sir.' The soldier was thanking her when she asked, 'Perhaps you could help me? If you climb to the top of this tree, you will find it is completely hollow. You will be able to drop right down inside. Here, tie this rope around your waist, so that I can lift you out again,' she said, passing the end of a coil of rope to him.

'Forgive me mistress, but why should I do such a thing?' the soldier asked politely.

So the witch explained, 'Below the tree is a hall with three rooms leading off from it. In the first room you will find a wooden chest, with a large dog sitting on the lid. His eyes are as large as saucers, but do not be afraid. Take my apron and spread it out on the floor. Place the dog on it, and he will sit quite calmly while you open the chest. It is full of copper pennies, and you may take as many as you like.'

The soldier hesitated, so the witch added cunningly, 'Of course, you might prefer *silver* coins. Enter the second room, and you will find another wooden chest in the centre. The dog sat upon it has eyes as large as millstones, but he is quite tame. Sit him on my apron and take as many coins as you like.'

The soldier brightened at the sound of so much silver, but then the witch said, 'If it's gold you prefer above all, enter the third room. The chest there is full of fine gold coins, and even though the dog that sits upon it has eyes wider than towers, you need not be afraid. Place him on my apron and fill your pockets with whatever you can carry.'

'This is all very well,' said the soldier suspiciously. 'But what is it that you want in return?'

The witch cackled, 'All I need is the tinderbox that you will find there. It was my grandmother's, and it is very dear to me. Promise that you'll bring it to me.'

The soldier promised and let the witch tie the rope around his waist. He then tucked her apron into his pocket, and climbed the tree. Just as the witch had described, the soldier dropped down inside the hollow tree and found himself in a brightly lit hall with three doors leading off it. The soldier opened the first door and saw the dog with eyes like saucers. He calmly laid the witch's apron out on the floor and lifted the dog down from the chest, so that he could look inside. He quickly filled his pockets with pennies, and lifted the dog back on to the chest before returning to the hall.

Now he tried the second room, and the dog with eyes as wide as millstones was much more terrifying than the first. He lifted it down on to the apron and opened the chest. Of course, the sight of the shining coins made the soldier empty his pockets of pennies and refill them with silver. Finally, he ventured into the third room, where the dog with eyes wider than towers sat. The soldier swallowed his fear and lifted it to the floor. There was so much gold inside the chest that he decided to leave the silver behind. He stuffed his pockets with as much gold as he could carry, then returned to the hall and called to the witch to pull him up. 'Do you have the tinderbox, sir?' she asked.

The soldier had forgotten it in his excitement, and went

back to get it before she hoisted him out of the hollow tree. 'Why is the tinderbox so important to you?' he asked.

'That's not your concern,' she snapped, and snatched the tinderbox. The soldier couldn't bear not knowing, so he threatened to cut off her head unless she explained. Still the witch refused. So the soldier drew his sword, chopped off her head in one blow, and took the box for himself.

The soldier was now richer than he had ever been. He set out for the nearest town and took a set of rooms at the finest inn there. He ate a delicious dinner, then had the best night's sleep he'd had in months. The next morning, the soldier marched out to buy himself some fine clothes. He quickly became known as a proper gentleman about the town, and everyone enjoyed visiting him. One day he heard the tale of the King's beautiful daughter, but was disappointed to discover that no one had ever seen her. It had been predicted that the Princess would marry an ordinary soldier, and her father refused to let her out of the castle in case it came true.

The soldier continued to enjoy his new wealth. He went to performances and attended grand dinners with his fine new friends. He gave money to the poor as often as possible, but all the while his thoughts wandered back to the Princess. *How could he meet her?*

Soon the soldier's grand new life reduced his supply of gold coins until he had almost nothing left. He was forced to move out of his expensive rooms, and his fine friends did not visit him any more. One night, as the last of his candles sputtered out, the soldier remembered the tinderbox. He struck the flint against the steel to get a spark of light, and at that instant the dog with eyes as large as saucers appeared at his side.

'What is your wish, sir?' the dog barked at him.

'Fetch me as many coins as you can carry,' he ordered. The dog ran off and returned with a bag full of copper pennies in his teeth. The soldier soon discovered that if he struck the flint twice, the second dog would appear. If he struck it three times, the third dog was instantly at his side. Soon the soldier returned to his expensive rooms, and his fine friends welcomed him back.

Now his money worries were over, the soldier's thoughts returned to the Princess. Suddenly it occurred to him that the tinderbox might hold the answer. He struck the flint once and when the first dog appeared he said, 'I would like to see the Princess.' The dog vanished at once and returned soon after with the Princess asleep on his back. She was just as beautiful as everyone had said, so the soldier leant forward to kiss her before the dog took her back.

The next day the Princess told everyone in the palace about her strange dream of a dog and a soldier. Her parents were most alarmed. They ordered a lady-in-waiting to stay by the Princess's bed until she awoke, to ensure that it was really just a dream. When the dog collected the Princess again that night, the lady followed him to the soldier's house. She marked a cross on the door of the house and left, but when the dog saw the cross, he marked another cross on every door in the town.

The King and Queen and their servants went to see the house where the Princess had been taken, but could not pick it out from all the crosses. The Queen refused to give up. She made a little bag out of a piece of silk and filled it with flour. She tied this around the Princess's neck and snipped a little hole in it. That night the dog collected the Princess again, but this time the flour left a trail behind them. It led right to the soldier's door. The next morning, he was thrown into the castle dungeons at once, where all he could do was think how very much he loved the Princess.

The soldier was told that he would be hanged the next day, and without the tinderbox there was nothing he could do. Early the next morning, before he was taken to the gallows, the soldier called out to a shoemaker's boy, who was passing the tiny window of his cell, 'Young man, if you bring me the tinderbox from the inn where I was staying, I will gladly pay you for it.' The boy did not need to be asked twice and ran as fast as he could to fetch it. When the soldier was led to the gallows, he held his head high. He asked for one last request – a pipe to smoke before he died. The King granted permission, and the soldier took out the tinderbox. He struck the flint first once, then twice, then three times.

The dog with eyes as large as saucers appeared, followed by the dog with eyes as wide as millstones. As soon as the dog with eyes wider than towers joined them, the soldier cried out, 'Help me!' The obedient creatures chased off the hangman and the crowd, even the King and Queen. They barked ferociously at anyone who came near, and the people were terrified. The soldier clearly had great power, and was asked to take over as King, for he was sure to protect the town well.

And so at last the Princess was able to come and go as she pleased, and, when the soldier asked her to marry him, she was very happy to become Queen. The celebrations lasted for days, and all the while the dogs with their huge eyes sat in attendance with them.

East Of The Sun, West Of The Moon

One autumn evening when a poor farmer and his children were gathered around a fire to keep warm, there came a knock at the door. The farmer opened it and to his surprise, a large white bear filled the doorway. The bear greeted him politely, and asked the farmer for his youngest girl, promising great riches in return.

The farmer did not say no straight away, and told the bear to come back a week later. He spent the days telling his daughter how wonderful things could be for her brothers and sisters. Reluctantly, the girl gave in. When the bear returned, the girl clambered onto his back with a small bundle of belongings in her hands, and they left.

After many hours, the two travellers reached a castle set high in the hills. It was gloriously decorated, with walls covered in tapestries and rich drapes at every door and window. Before he left her alone the bear gave the girl a bell, and said that she had only to ring it if she needed anything at all. She felt hungry after the journey, so she rang the bell to ask for a meal. It had barely rung once when a feast appeared before her. When she had eaten, she felt quite tired. She rang the bell again, and was transported to a beautiful bedchamber, high in a turret.

As the girl blew out her light the door creaked open. A young man came in, laid down by the fire, and went to sleep. The surprised girl had no idea that this was really the white bear who had brought her there. He was an enchanted Prince, and could only return to his human form at night.

For many days and nights this routine continued. The girl spent each day wandering the castle alone, and each night wondering who slept by the fire. She found that she hated being alone so often, and told the bear that she wished to visit her family.

'Promise you will not speak with your mother alone, and I shall happily take you,' said the bear. 'But if you break this promise and tell her anything at all, everything will be ruined for us both.' So, after many hours travelling, they arrived at the large farmhouse where her family now lived. The bear reminded the girl of her promise, and left.

Everyone asked dozens of questions about her new life. She answered as well as she could, and it was not until much later that the girl accidentally found herself alone with her mother. The poor girl could not help but tell her everything about life at the castle. 'Oh, but you are probably living with an ugly troll,' exclaimed her mother. 'Hide this candle in your pocket. While he sleeps you will be able to see him by it, but take care not to spill any wax on him, or he will know what you have done.'

When the bear came to take her home, the girl admitted she had spoken with her mother alone. 'Then everything will be ruined for us both,' the bear replied sadly. The girl felt sure that if she was careful, nothing could go wrong.

That night, she lit the candle to discover who slept by the fire. Rather than a troll, she saw a handsome prince. She fell instantly in love and, as he looked so peaceful, leant forward to kiss his cheek. Three drops of hot wax fell from her candle onto his shirt. The Prince woke with a start, and cried, 'What have you done? My stepmother's spell would have been broken if you had just waited a year. Now I must go to her castle, east of the sun and west of the moon, to marry Princess Long-Nose. Everything is ruined for us both!'

The next day the Prince and the castle had both vanished, and the girl was alone. She walked for days, until she reached

the base of a large mountain. There sat an old woman playing with a golden apple. 'Do you know the way to the castle east of the sun and west of the moon?' asked the girl.

The woman shook her head. 'I only know it is very far from here, and the Prince is to marry Princess Long-Nose, but perhaps it is you who should marry him? I shall lend you my horse to ride to my neighbour. She might be able to help you. Please take this golden apple; it may be useful to you.'

The girl thanked the woman and rode away. In the next valley, a woman was sitting outside her house using a golden carding comb to prepare some wool for spinning. 'Excuse me, do you know the way to the castle east of the sun and west of the moon?' asked the girl.

'I only know that it is very far from here,' the woman replied. 'I can lend you my horse to ride to my friend. She may help. Take my carding comb; it may be useful to you.'

The girl rode to a third house, where a woman sat using a golden spinning wheel. 'Do you know the way to the castle east of the sun and west of the moon?' the girl asked.

'I only know that it is very far from here,' came the reply. 'The Prince who lives there is to marry Princess Long-Nose. Perhaps it is you who should marry him though?' the woman asked. So she lent the girl her horse and gave her the golden spinning wheel, instructing her to ride to the East Wind, who may be able to take her to the castle.

When the girl found the East Wind, she asked if he could show her the way to the castle east of the sun and west of the moon. 'I cannot,' said the East Wind. 'I have never blown so far, but the West Wind may know the way. I will take you to him.' The East Wind carried the girl on his back to meet his brother, the West Wind. When they arrived, he told her story, and asked if he knew the way.

'I do not,' said the West Wind. 'For I have never blown so

far, but the South Wind may know; he is stronger than both of us. I will take you to him.'

The West Wind told her story as soon as they arrived, and asked if the South Wind knew the way to the castle. Even the South Wind, who had blown to many far-flung places, had never come across it. He felt sure however, that his brother, the North Wind would know and offered to take her to him. So the girl rode on his back to the home of the North Wind, where the air was so cold it would freeze the hair on your head. Over the North Wind's howling, the South Wind explained the girl's story. 'Have you ever seen the castle east of the sun and west of the moon?'

The North Wind howled, 'Oh yes. I had blown for many days, and had almost no breath left at all when I reached it, but if you have the courage to come with me to find the Prince, I will take you there.'

So the girl climbed on to the North Wind's back, and he drew in a breath so huge that the air around them rumbled. The North Wind blew and blew, over mountains and forests, towns and villages, until he had almost no breath left at all. He had only just enough strength to drop the girl at the gates of the castle. She settled on the grass in front of a window and took the golden apple from her pocket. She threw it into the air, so that it caught the light prettily. A Princess with a very long nose leant out of the window. 'What do you want in exchange for that apple?' she asked.

The girl thought for a moment, then said, 'If you allow me to visit the Prince, I'll gladly give it to you.' The Princess agreed and took the apple. She knew that the Prince would not be awake to see the girl. Sure enough, nothing the girl did woke the Prince, and in the morning the Princess sent her away.

The next day, the girl sat in front of the window, and used the golden carding comb. Again, the Princess asked her for it in exchange for a visit to the Prince, but the girl couldn't wake him. The day after that, she used the golden spinning wheel in front of the window. When Princess Long-Nose offered money for it, the girl asked to visit the Prince again.

The Prince, meanwhile, had no idea that the girl he loved had visited him until some kind people who had overheard

her attempts to wake him told him of her visits. He
realized that the Princess must be drugging him at night.
That evening, the Prince pretended to swallow her sleeping
potion and to fall asleep as he had before. This time when
the girl came to visit him, the Prince awoke immediately.
'I must marry Princess Long-Nose tomorrow unless you can
save me,' he whispered. 'I will say that I can only marry
the person who can wash the drops of wax from my shirt.
You are the only one who will be able to do this, as it was
you who spilled the wax.

In the morning, the Prince announced his request to
Princess Long-Nose and her troll-mother. They were sure it
would be a simple thing to do and agreed. The Princess
plunged the shirt into a pot of water and scrubbed at the
drops of wax. She scrubbed and scrubbed, but the drops of
wax simply grew larger and darker until the shirt looked
completely ruined. 'You girl!' the Prince called to the girl,
who had waited outside the open window once more. 'Can
you get this shirt clean again? Princess Long-Nose has done
a terrible job, and I'm certain you can do it better.'

The girl smiled, and said that she would try her best. She
plunged the shirt into the pot of water, and it came out
completely clean. The Prince laughed, delighted at the
sight of the shocked faces around him. 'This is the girl
I will marry,' he said, smiling down at her.

Thumbelina

A woman once visited a fairy and asked her to grant her wish for a child. She was given a magical barleycorn to take home, and as soon as it was planted it grew into a tiny flower bud. The woman kissed the tip of the flower bud sadly and, to her surprise, it blossomed. Inside the petals sat a tiny girl, the size of a thumb. The woman named her Thumbelina and made her a little bed from a walnut shell. She filled it with violet petals for a soft mattress, with a velvety rose petal for a quilt.

Thumbelina spent her days rowing around a water-filled plate in a floating tulip petal, singing to her mother. One day, a fat, wet lady toad, heard Thumbelina singing. She waited until the tiny girl fell asleep, then hopped in through a window. When the toad saw Thumbelina, she knew that she had found the perfect wife for her son. She picked her up, walnut and all, and took her to the edge of the stream in the garden. Her son croaked loudly when he saw the tiny girl, but his mother hushed him. 'I'll put her on a lily pad so she cannot run away,' the old toad decided. And she swam Thumbelina in her walnut shell out into the stream.

When she awoke, Thumbelina found herself all alone on the lily pad, with no idea how she had got there. The two toads swam over to greet her, and she was terribly upset to learn that she was to marry the ugly young son. He simply croaked at her. The two toads took away Thumbelina's walnut-shell bed and left her all alone on the lily pad.

Poor Thumbelina sat and wept. The sound of her tears carried to the fish in the water below who had all heard the toads' plan. They peeped above the surface to see and could not bear to think of such a beautiful girl living with toads. So they nibbled away at the stalk of the lily pad until it floated free. Thumbelina was soon sailing downstream, far out of reach of the toads.

As she floated by, all the creatures in the trees by the stream admired Thumbelina. A butterfly fluttered around her head and landed on the lily pad. Thumbelina thought the butterfly was very pretty, so she fastened one end of a ribbon to its leg and the other to the lily pad. A large beetle flying overhead spotted the tiny girl and swooped at her. He grabbed her by her waist and took her back to his tree by the water, leaving the poor butterfly still attached to the lily pad sailing away downstream. Poor Thumbelina.

The beetles were very unkind to her, and she felt badly for the butterfly, who must still be tied to the lily pad. The beetle soon lost interest and flew her back to the ground. He left her in the grass, and Thumbelina spent the summer living in the shade of a large buttercup. She did very well indeed, but when winter arrived the buttercup withered, and there was nowhere to shelter from the snow.

Thumbelina couldn't stay where she was, so she walked away from the woods until she reached a cornfield. There she found the tiny home of a fieldmouse, who had made the place very cosy for winter. 'I'm so cold and hungry,' said Thumbelina. 'Could you spare a piece of barleycorn?' The fieldmouse took pity on the tiny girl and took her in.

The two were soon visited by a mole who was the fieldmouse's friend. He was quite blind, but fell in love with Thumbelina's beautiful voice. 'You are welcome to visit me as often as you please, Thumbelina' he said.

Thumbelina and the fieldmouse often visited the mole through a tunnel he had dug between their two homes. One day they found that a swallow had crept inside the tunnel and died from the cold. 'How sad,' thought Thumbelina, for she loved how the birds sang all summer. The poor swallow should have flown somewhere warmer before winter had set in. Thumbelina felt so badly for the

swallow that she could not sleep. So she made him a blanket woven from hay, and lined with tufts of wool and flower down. To her surprise, when she laid the blanket over the bird, she could feel his heart still beating. The warmth of the blanket had revived him.

The next day the swallow opened his eyes and thanked Thumbelina for saving his life. The poor bird had hurt his wing and hadn't been able to keep up with the other swallows. Thumbelina promised to take care of him until spring came and the weather was warm again.

Thumbelina fetched him water in the cup of a petal, and kept him secret from the fieldmouse and the mole, who did not like birds. When the weather was warmer, she opened up one of the holes the mole had made and let the swallow out. 'Come with me, Thumbelina,' he begged. But Thumbelina wouldn't leave without saying goodbye to the fieldmouse, and the swallow flew sadly away.

The corn grew strong and tall again, and the fieldmouse soon announced to Thumbelina that the mole would like to marry her. Poor Thumbelina couldn't think of an excuse not to marry the pompous old mole, and the wedding arrangements began. She was to have the finest clothes and a home, but she would never live above ground again. Thumbelina wept, because she would not see the world

anymore. As autumn took over from summer, she went above the ground as often as she could. One last time she said goodbye to the sun. Just as Thumbelina turned to go back inside, she heard the wonderful sound of the swallow singing above her. He flew down to greet her, and Thumbelina told him all about the wedding the fieldmouse and the mole were planning. She began to weep again.

'Thumbelina, you rescued me from the cold winter, won't you come with me this time? I'll take you far from here where the weather is warm, and the flowers blossom all winter. You should not have to live underground – you'll be too sad. Let me help you.' Thumbelina agreed. She hopped on to the swallow, and secured herself by tying her ribbon belt to one of his feathers. The swallow soared into the sky with the tiny girl safe in the warm feathers on his back.

Thumbelina gazed in wonder as they passed over the snowy mountains and great forests below. They came at last to a place where the sunlight was dazzlingly bright, and the sky so blue it was breathtaking. The swallow headed for the ruins of an ancient palace that stood by a lake. At the top of the ruins was the swallow's nest, but he knew that Thumbelina would not be happy living there. He carried her down to the beautiful white blossoms of a vine growing up the ruins, and let her out onto a leaf. A tiny winged man wearing a golden crown appeared from inside one of the

flowers. He was surprised to see such a beautiful girl
accompanied by an enormous bird. Thumbelina was just as
surprised to discover that there were other people just like
her. 'He's so handsome,' she whispered to the swallow.

The man thought she was the most beautiful girl he had
ever seen, and placed his crown upon Thumbelina's head.
'Would you marry me?' he asked the stunned girl.

'Yes,' she said at once. As other tiny men and women
emerged from the surrounding flowers, Thumbelina knew
she would be happy there. One tiny woman brought her a
beautiful pair of wings, which she put straight on, so that
she could fly around just like the others. The swallow sang
a beautiful song for their wedding, and Thumbelina was
renamed Maia, a fairy name. Each winter when he escaped
the cold, the swallow visited his friend and her new family,
safe in the knowledge that Thumbelina was happy at last.

Rumpelstiltskin

There was once a miller who could not resist boasting, even if the things he said were not true. One day he bragged that his daughter, Louisa, could spin straw into gold. The King came to hear of this and ordered the miller to bring Louisa to the castle at once.

When they arrived at the castle, the King led Louisa to a room in a tower. It was full of straw with a spinning wheel in the middle. 'You have the whole night to spin this straw into gold for me,' the King announced, clapping his hands. 'But if you don't finish it all, you will die.' He closed the door and left Louisa all alone.

The miller was horrified, and Louisa, who had no idea how to spin straw into gold, put her head in her hands in despair. Suddenly the door swung open. A little man stepped into the room. 'Why are you crying so, young maid?' he asked the girl.

The miller's daughter looked up, and through her tears she said, 'I'm supposed to spin all of the straw in this room into gold, and I have no idea how to do it.'

The man looked at her thoughtfully and said, 'If I spin the straw for you, what will you give me in exchange?'

'This necklace, if you'll have it,' said the girl hopefully.

The man nodded in agreement and set to work. By morning the straw had all been turned into gold. The King's eyes lit up with greed. The girl was taken to another room with even more straw, and the little man appeared again. This time he took the girl's ring in exchange and spun the wheel all night through. In the morning the room was full of gold. The King was delighted by the sight and had the poor girl taken to a third room full of straw.

'If you spin all of this straw into gold by morning, I shall gladly make you my wife,' he said. He would be richer than any other king, with Louisa as his Queen.

When the little man appeared, the girl could not offer him anything else in exchange for spinning the straw into gold. The man smiled and asked, 'If I spin the straw into gold, you will become Queen?' The girl nodded and he said,

'Promise to give me your first child, and I'll gladly spin the straw for you.' The miller's daughter promised, as she could see no way around it, and the man spun the straw into gold for her. The King married her the very next day.

A year later, the Queen had a baby boy. She did not even think of the promise she had made until the little man appeared before her. When he demanded that she give him the baby, the Queen begged him to take anything else he could wish for. The man sighed, and began to feel sorry for her after all. 'I'll give you three days. If you can guess what my name is when I return, you may keep the child.'

The Queen racked her brain for all the names she could think of, and sent a servant to search for the most unusual names he could find. When the little man visited the next day she listed each one for him. None of them was right.

The Queen spent the next day making a list of more names. Each one was wrong, and she feared for her baby. When the servant returned on the morning of the third day, he had no new names, but he did have a strange story to tell. 'Your Majesty,' he said. 'I came across a small house in the forest. In front of it a little man was dancing around a fire, singing:

"The fire is hot, the weather is fine,
The royal child will soon be mine.

The Queen will never guess this game
For Rumpelstiltskin is my name!" '

This was surely the man who could spin straw into gold.
When he came that evening he said, 'Let's see if you can
guess my name at last.'

The Queen smiled and said, 'Is it Rumpelstiltskin?'

'H-how?' he spluttered. 'How did you discover it? No, no,
NO!' He flew into a rage and stomped his foot with such
force that he disappeared into the floor and was no more.

The Nightingale

Long ago in China lived an Emperor whose palace was so glorious that everyone who visited could not help but admire it. It was built entirely of porcelain, and each step that people took resounded like the ringing of beautiful bells. The garden was filled with the most wonderful plants from around the world, and beyond the walls lay a forest containing the finest trees in the Empire.

It was said that a Nightingale lived in the forest, whose song was so sweet it brought a tear to the eye of everyone who heard it. Fishermen would stop their work to listen, and every visitor said that the Nightingale was the very best thing about their stay.

Poems and books were written about the Nightingale, and the Emperor himself came to hear of it. 'Have you seen this bird?' he asked a courtier.

'No, your Majesty, it has not been at court, but I will find it for you.' The courtier went about the palace, and asked everyone if they had seen the Nightingale. It was not until he came to the kitchens that a young serving girl said she often heard the Nightingale sing when she visited her sick mother. The courtier told the girl to take him there, and

everyone from the palace followed,
anxious to please their Emperor.

Along the way, a cow began to low, and
everyone there murmured at the lovely
sound. 'That is only a cow lowing,' said the girl and
kept walking. Next they heard the sound of frogs
croaking, and the people said how beautiful the
Nightingale sounded. 'But those are just the frogs in the
marshes,' said the girl. 'It is further yet.' At last a beautiful
singing was heard through the trees and tears came to the
eyes of everyone present. The girl halted and held out her
arm, pointing through the trees to the bird's hiding place.
'There,' she said. A small mud-coloured bird was sitting on the
branch of a tree. She called to it, 'Nightingale, the Emperor
would love to hear you sing. Will you please come to court
this evening?'

'Of course,' sang the bird, and set off for the palace with them.

That evening the entire court was present to hear the little
bird sing. As it began, the sound so moved the Emperor that
tears welled up in his eyes. He declared that the Nightingale
should be given his favourite golden slippers, but the bird
refused, saying that seeing the Emperor so moved by her
singing was thanks enough. So the Nightingale was given a
cage at court and its own servants. It was let out twice each

day and once each evening, with one of her servants always keeping her on a long silken thread. Flying about was never as enjoyable after that.

A few weeks later, a large package arrived from the Emperor of Japan, labelled 'The Nightingale'. Inside was a small chest containing a beautiful clockwork bird, covered in jewels. When it was wound, the bird sang out just like the real Nightingale, except that it never grew tired and was much lovelier to look at. Its pretty tune was played over and over again for days. No one noticed that the real Nightingale had vanished until the Emperor asked to hear it sing again, but it was nowhere to be found. The clockwork bird was so popular that no one minded, and it took pride of place at the Emperor's bedside.

For a year everyone admired the clockwork bird, and the pretty tune it sang, until one night, as the Emperor lay in bed, humming along with the bird, a strange clicking sound echoed inside it. The clicking was followed by an alarming whirring noise that drowned out the tune, and then the clockwork bird went completely silent. The Emperor was beside himself. He sent for a courtier, who sent for the clock-maker. The clock-maker declared that the bird was quite worn out – it should only be played once a year, or it would be damaged beyond repair.

As the years passed by a terrible sadness came over the Emperor. He became so unwell that a new emperor was chosen to replace him. The old Emperor became so still in his bed that everyone assumed he was dead, and they went away to honour his replacement. When he awoke, the Emperor was quite alone, and he started to think of everything he had done in his life. He cried out for music to distract himself, but although moonlight shone prettily on the clockwork bird's jewels, there was no one there to wind it. The Emperor lay in silence, lost in his thoughts.

At last, the sound of such sweet singing came through the open window that tears came to the Emperor's eyes. The little Nightingale had heard of his illness and had come to give him what comfort it could. The joy of hearing the little bird sing again made the Emperor feel so much better that he sat up slightly in his bed and even smiled. 'Thank you, little bird,' he whispered through his tears. 'How can I ever repay you for coming back to me in my time of need?'

'Your tears are thanks enough, Emperor,' said the Nightingale, and it sang the Emperor into a restful sleep. When he awoke, the sun was shining and the Nightingale was still by his side, although none of his courtiers had returned to check on him, for they all believed he was dead. 'I will visit you each evening and tell you everything that I have heard,' promised the Nightingale, 'but please don't put me in a cage again. I need to fly freely, and build

my nest out in the forest that is my home.' The Nightingale asked for just one more thing in return for its visits. 'You must keep the news of my return a secret. No one must know that a little bird brings you all the secrets of the Empire,' said the Nightingale. The Emperor promised these things faithfully with his hand over his heart. The little bird flew off just as the bedroom door opened wide.

'Good morning!' cried the Emperor cheerfully from his bed to a group of very surprised courtiers. They could not believe he was alive and gathered around him in relief.

The Brave Little Tailor

There was once a tailor who would sit at his window each day stitching fine garments for the people of his town. One day as he worked, the tailor heard the cry of a jam-seller on the street. He called her over to buy a pot, paid the woman, and set to spreading a portion of jam on a thick slice of bread.

Now the tailor did not wish to ruin the garment that he was sewing, so he set the bread aside while he finished. As he pinned and stitched, the tailor noticed the sweet smell of jam was drawing in flies. They hovered and buzzed over his delicious snack, making him quite cross. He picked up a piece of cloth, and took one great swipe at the persistent insects. To his astonishment, seven flies lay dead at his feet. 'Seven with one blow?' he thought. 'That is unbelievable. I should go out and tell people what I have done.'

So the little tailor embroidered himself a sash, proudly proclaiming, 'Seven in one blow.' He looked for supplies to take on his journey, but all he had was a piece of soft cheese. He put it in his pocket, and set off to show the world how very brave he was.

Just outside his house, the tailor noticed a small bird, caught up in the bushes. He untangled it and placed it in his pocket to recover. The tailor started walking up the mountain road and soon came upon a grumpy giant. The giant looked quite unimpressed with the tailor until he displayed his sash to him. 'Seven in one blow?' the giant thought, surprised that such a little fellow had beaten seven men at once. He decided to set the man a challenge, and squeezed a small rock until several drops of water fell from it to the ground. He then asked, 'Can you do better?'

The tailor took the cheese from his pocket. Pretending it was a normal rock, he cried, 'That's nothing,' and squeezed until all its liquid ran out. The furious giant chose another rock and threw it so high into the air that it became a tiny speck in the distance. In reply, the tailor took the bird from his pocket and flung it into the sky. The creature, happy to be released, flew out of sight and did not come back.

'You can throw well enough,' said the giant, grudgingly, 'but are you strong enough to carry this tree with me?' The tailor allowed the giant to pick up the trunk, but instead of helping, he settled himself on one of the branches, while the giant took the weight of the whole tree. When the giant became exhausted and dropped the tree, the tailor simply hopped down laughing and pretended to have helped all along.

The pair walked a little way together and came to an orchard. The giant kindly bent the branches of a cherry tree

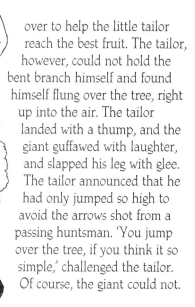

over to help the little tailor reach the best fruit. The tailor, however, could not hold the bent branch himself and found himself flung over the tree, right up into the air. The tailor landed with a thump, and the giant guffawed with laughter, and slapped his leg with glee. The tailor announced that he had only jumped so high to avoid the arrows shot from a passing huntsman. 'You jump over the tree, if you think it so simple,' challenged the tailor. Of course, the giant could not.

Outraged, the giant roared, 'If you are so very brave, you will spend the night with us giants.' The tailor agreed, and the giant showed him to a bed while the other giants settled around a fire. As the bed was so big, the tailor huddled into a corner for warmth, so when the giant angrily broke the bed in two he missed the sleeping tailor completely. When the tailor joined them for breakfast in the morning, still in one piece, the terrified giants hurried off before he could hurt them.

The tailor continued proudly on his journey. When he began to feel quite tired, he found a comfortable spot to rest in a royal courtyard. While he slept, people gathered round to see who he was. They saw his sash and exclaimed at his bravery. He was soon mentioned to the King. The King sent a messenger to speak with the tailor when he awoke, who offered him fine lodgings if he would join the King's guard. However, the other soldiers were horrified, and begged to be excused from the King's service rather than look weak in comparison to the little man.

The King, for his part, was horrified to lose such loyal men, and racked his brains for a way to get rid of the tailor. So he set the tailor a series of challenges, offering his daughter's hand in marriage, and half his kingdom, as a prize.

First, he was asked to rid the kingdom of two troublesome giants that lived in the forest. This was simple for such a brave man, so the tailor asked the soldiers to wait while he went into the forest alone. The giants were asleep beneath a tree. The tailor gathered some stones and climbed up above them. He dropped the stones one by one, hitting the giants repeatedly on their heads. Both awoke with deafening roars. 'Why are you hitting me?' demanded one.

'How dare you? It is you that hit me,' cried the other. They set upon each other in such a rage that it was not long before they both lay dead on the ground. The little tailor leapt down and ran each of the giants through with his sword for good measure, before returning to the waiting soldiers to tell them of his success.

The King's next challenge for the tailor was to capture a unicorn that was causing the kingdom many problems. The tailor left the soldiers at the edge of the forest once more and set off with just a length of rope and an axe to hunt the beast. When he found the unicorn, it rushed straight at him, meaning to catch him on the point of its horn.

The tailor bravely stood his ground until the last moment, then leapt aside, so that its horn drove straight into the trunk of a tree. He tethered the unicorn with the rope he had brought, then carefully chopped away the wood around its horn to prise it loose.

The King was astonished that the little tailor had accomplished such a challenge, but was still reluctant to give in. He set what he thought would be the hardest challenge yet. He asked the tailor to bring him a violent wild boar that roamed the forest. The boar brought misery to all the nearby farmers, so the soldiers were relieved when the tailor again refused their help and set off alone.

The moment the boar spotted the tailor, it ran right at him, and the brave little man was forced to act quickly. He ran into a nearby church and leapt out of a window. The boar followed him inside and, quick as a flash, the tailor rushed to the door, and shut the angry beast inside. The boar was trapped. Now the tailor could marry the King's daughter and rule half the kingdom – he was crowned King.

One night the young Queen heard her husband chattering in his sleep. She realized that she was not married to a brave soldier, as she had thought, but to a humble tailor. She was outraged and went to her father for help. The King told her to leave their chamber door ajar that evening. He then ordered his men to kidnap the tailor and put him on a ship that very night, so that he would never be able to bother them again.

It was most fortunate for the tailor that among the King's men he had a true friend, who warned him of the plot against him. So that evening, the tailor went to bed as normal, but only pretended to sleep. Just as the men were about to drag him off, the tailor started to mumble as though he was chattering in his sleep again. 'Fetch me the shears and finish that seam boy, or I will box your ears! I conquered seven in one blow, killed two giants, caught a unicorn and trapped one wild boar – I have no fear of the men coming to get me.'

At that, the men ran off, far too terrified to try to take the tailor away. The tailor's reputation grew and grew until no one in the kingdom was prepared to challenge him, and so he remained King for the rest of his days.

The Snow Queen

A girl and a boy, named Gerda and Kay, were once the best of friends. They were poor, but happy, and lived in houses so close together that they could hold hands across the open windows. They would sit under the window-box rose bushes, while Kay's grandmother told stories. One day, while the snow flurried around in the sky like little white bees, she told them of the Queen of the snowflakes.

The Snow Queen, she said, lived in the far north, only coming south to bring the cold weather with her. This cold had once shattered an evil hobgoblin's mirror, and even now its fragments caused trouble around the world.

As his grandmother spoke, a tiny grain of glass from the hobgoblin's mirror flew into poor Kay's eye. A sliver of glass settled in his heart, and life changed forever. He became a very different boy, for each piece of mirror had a terrible effect. He became cruel and cold, and his friendship with little Gerda was shattered like the mirror.

Kay left Gerda alone and went to play with the other boys who would hitch their sleds to people's carriages and ride along in the snow. Kay hitched his sled to a glorious-looking carriage, and it did not stop. The driver was the Snow Queen herself, and she refused to leave Kay behind.

For days, Gerda worried that something may have happened to Kay. So she decided to go in search of him. She asked everyone she met if they had seen her friend, and even went to the river to ask the waves if they had seen him. The waves seemed to be nodding up and down, so Gerda stepped into a boat, to search downstream. She pushed off from the bank, and found herself floating away from home, and away from everything she knew. As she sailed along, Gerda called out to the willow trees and the birds, asking each of them if they had seen her friend, Kay. 'No,' they all replied.

After several hours, Gerda spotted an orchard by the side of the river. An old woman sat in a cottage doorway wearing a flowered sunhat, so Gerda called out to attract her attention. She pulled Gerda's boat into shore and lifted the girl on to dry land. 'How did you come to be floating downstream all alone?' asked the woman. Gerda told her tale and asked if she had seen her friend, Kay. The woman had not, but she took a liking to young Gerda, and wanted her to stay. She took her magic brush and untangled Gerda's hair.

As the old woman brushed, the little girl forgot how urgent her journey was, and began to enjoy the warmth of the sunshine instead. The woman carefully removed the roses from her garden, in case Gerda should see them and be reminded of home. It was not until Gerda saw the pretty

little roses on the woman's sunhat that she began to remember her quest to find Kay. Gerda ran out of the garden and through the orchard as fast as she could.

So much time had passed that it was now autumn, and she wept for the time she had wasted. Even though she was cold and upset, young Gerda dried her tears and opened her eyes. There sat a crow. He cawed at her and asked what was wrong, so Gerda told her tale. She asked the crow if he might have seen her friend, Kay. To her surprise the crow cawed, 'Yes, I think I might. My wife lives in the palace kitchens. She has told me such exciting things about the Princess's recent wedding.'

'Yes?' asked Gerda, anxious for news.

The crow described a lavish ceremony; the Princess's gown, and, finally, a young man just like Kay. Gerda was so excited that she begged the crow to help her gain entry to the palace. So he led the way to the palace gardens, where they met his wife. She showed them into the palace, hushing them to be as quiet as mice. They tiptoed through a series of beautifully decorated chambers, but Gerda hardly noticed a thing — she was anxious to see her friend.

At last, the crow's wife led them to a bedchamber. In it were two pretty beds in the shape of flowers: one white,

one red. When she peeped inside the white bed, Gerda spied a young Princess, sleeping happily. She turned to the red bed, holding her breath, and peeped inside. She saw a handsome young man, but it was not Kay. Gerda sobbed so loudly that the Prince and Princess woke right up. 'Whatever is the matter?' enquired the Princess, so Gerda told her tale once more. They asked if they could help her. Gerda asked for nothing more than warm clothes to see her through winter. To her surprise, she was given a fine carriage made of gold, as well as a thick coat, boots, and a muff to warm her hands. Quickly she set off to continue her search.

The crow travelled with his new friend for a few miles, then said a fond farewell at the edge of a forest. Not two miles into the trees, a group of robbers lay in wait. When they saw the carriage driving towards them, they could not believe their luck, and stepped out in front of it. Gerda was terrified, but the robbers' daughter took pity on her. She thought that Gerda would make a good companion, and stopped her mother from cutting off her head.

The robber girl was a bossy young thing who always got her way. She insisted on driving the carriage back to the robbers' lair herself, with Gerda at her side. As they drove,

Gerda told her tale again, but the robber girl would not let her go. Instead they ate a large supper, then lay down in a pile of furs under the watchful eyes of the robber girl's frightened birds and reindeer. She slipped her knife under her pillow, and made poor Gerda tell her tale once more. It made a strange bedtime story, but she was soon asleep.

Poor Gerda lay wide awake, worrying about Kay. Above her head the pigeons cooed quietly. 'We have seen your young friend, Kay,' they seemed to say. 'The Snow Queen took him north in the spring.'

'Oh, yes,' sighed a reindeer, who was huddled in the corner, away from the robber girl's knife. 'It is a wonderful place where you can run for miles in crisp, fresh snow.' He sighed again. Gerda could hardly lie still in her excitement.

In the morning the little robber girl, who had a kind heart, offered to let Gerda go. She gave up her reindeer, and gave back Gerda's boots, but could not bear to part with the

warmth of the muff, so she handed over her mother's warmest mittens instead. Gerda waved farewell, and she and the reindeer headed north. They soon caught sight of the colourful Northern Lights, weaving their magical rainbow across the night sky. Gerda thought she had never seen anything quite so beautiful, and huddled into the reindeer's neck happily as he ran. She was sure that she would soon see Kay again.

They stopped to rest at the house of an old Laplander, a woman the reindeer knew well, who shared her meal and the heat of her fire with them, and listened while Gerda told her tale. 'I know of the Snow Queen's palace,' she said thoughtfully, 'but it is still very far from here.' So she gave directions to her cousin's house, further north in Finland, and sent them on their way. When they arrived at the old Finlander's home, she welcomed them happily and listened to their tale intently. Gerda's reindeer friend begged the old Finlander to make the young girl as powerful as possible, so that she might rescue her friend, Kay.

The wise Finlander smiled at them both. 'Have you not noticed how well Gerda has done by herself? She has all the power she needs. She simply needs to find a way to remove the sliver of glass from her friend's eye and the sliver of glass from his heart. Until that is done, he will never see the truth about the Snow Queen. He will be happy to stay with her forever.'

The Finlander sent her friends out to the edge of the Snow Queen's domain, where the reindeer set Gerda down. 'You must carry on alone, Gerda,' he whispered, 'but I will wait for you here.' As the young girl stepped bravely forwards, a storm of snowflakes swooped around her. Each flake grew and grew until it was the size of a human soldier. Gerda ran, and as she ran the steam from her breath expanded and became an army of protective angels. They pushed back the advancing soldiers, so that she could reach the Snow Queen's palace.

Little Kay, meanwhile, had spent many months as the companion of the Snow Queen. His lips were quite blue, for the palace was made entirely of ice and snow, but Kay did not seem to notice. The palace shone with the rainbow lights from the sky, and at the centre of it was a glittering frozen lake. In the middle of this lake sat the Snow Queen, raised high on her beautiful throne. By her side, sat young Kay, who smiled up at her adoringly, shivering all the while. With winter approaching in the south, it was time for the Snow Queen to travel there and wreak her havoc, as she did every year. She left Kay struggling over an impossible puzzle to keep him occupied until her return, then swept out of the palace with a cold blast of air. Kay was in such deep concentration that he did not even notice when Gerda came towards him across the ice. He still didn't notice when she pulled him into her arms, and even when she called his name.

Poor Gerda wept for him. Her hot tears spilled on to his heart, washing away the sliver of glass. Kay looked up at his old friend and began to cry himself. The sliver of glass lodged in his eye was swept away, and he saw clearly for the first time in months. He hugged her back with all his strength, and the two of them ran out of the palace before anyone could see them. The reindeer was waiting, and he carefully carried them back to their homes, while they laughed with joy, impatient to see their families again.

THE END

ALSO AVAILABLE:

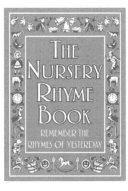

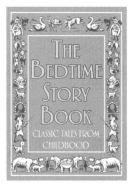

The Nursery Rhyme Book £5.00
ISBN: 978-1-84317-307-6

The Bedtime Story Book £5.00
ISBN: 978-1-84317-336-6

If you would like to order this book please contact:
Bookpost, PO Box 29, Douglas, Isle of Man, IM99 1BQ
Tel. 01624 677237 Fax 01624 670923